I0631538

Ohh! Gods are Online..

Ohh! Gods are Online..

A magical tale of real Gods,
corrupt men and virtual worlds

Rashma N. Kalsie
George Dixon

Srishti
PUBLISHERS & DISTRIBUTORS

SRISHTI PUBLISHERS & DISTRIBUTORS
N-16, C. R. Park
New Delhi 110 019
editorial@srishtipublishers.com

First published by
Srishti Publishers & Distributors in 2013

Copyright © Rashma N. Kalsie and George Dixon, 2013

The author asserts the moral right to be identified as the author of this work.

Typeset by EGP at Srishti

All rights reserved. No part of this publication may be reproduced, stored in a retrieval system, or transmitted, in any form or by any means, electronic, mechanical, photocopying, recording or otherwise, without the prior written permission of the Publishers.

This is a work of fiction. Names, characters, places and incidents are either products of the author's imagination or used fictitiously. Any resemblance to actual events, locales or persons, living or dead, is entirely coincidental.

Dedication

I dedicate my first book to my parents, who struggled to domesticate me, till they realized it was an exercise in futility, and then became my biggest support system.

−Rashma

I dedicate this book to my children and to my wife who I love immensely. To my Father, who is now living in his own personal Heaven and to my Mother who is still in this world although, I am sure has some sort of influence on the Gods in their worlds.

− Phil Cherry

ACKNOWLEDGEMENTS

৪১

Rashma

I am grateful to the teams at Srishti for believing in the story and the 'worlds' we created. I am also grateful to Phil Cherry, the co-author of my debut novel, for putting up with my autocratic behaviour. But for him half the book wouldn't have been written. My salaams to Jehanara and her editorial team for giving the book the finish it lacked when it was handed over to them for editing. A special mention of Dr. Bharat Gupt, a mentor and a friend, who has helped me come to my own as a writer and a playwright. It will be unbecoming to not acknowledge my husband who has paid my bills for many years in the hope that I will write a best seller some day. And last of all an express of gratitude to my friend and teacher, Karen Phebe, who gave me a constructive feedback and to Ken, for telling me I had what it takes to be a successful writer.

Phil Cherry

I am very grateful to the teams at Srishti for having faith in the story and the rippling worlds of the Gods that myself and my co-author have created in our story. I am also extremely lucky to have met my co- author over the internet and I am grateful to her for pushing me when I was at a low ebb, so as to get this novel completed. She is a bully when it comes to my laziness and I feel that without her hard work, not only on the writing side but also in the fact that she kept me fascinated with the script, that this novel would never have been finished. My thanks also go out to Jehanara and her team who gave the work the polish that it needed. I also wish to thank my wife for her ongoing faith in me as I typed away on my own in another room and left her alone to get on with the domestic part of our existence. So many other people have had faith in me and I thank them too, especially the ones that have bought my other published works. It seems that I have a little following and I am happy that people appreciate what I have contributed towards the written word. I also hope that anyone who reads this work feels that they too have a story to tell and that this small work helps to enable them to write it.

CHRIST

૪૭

It was warm here. Warm and wet, in a nice way though. The new life had been cooking gently in the moisture that protects this new life for some time now. It had grown naturally, fed from the moisture that had been provided. It grew, and as it grew, it aged, unknowing that it was in fact growing bigger by the minute.

This was nature's way of course and no one questioned it. The new life was by now big enough to break free from its confines. It was time it 'branched out on its own', thought the new life force. It started to attack its surroundings even though it was these very surroundings that had protected it for so long.

The Hen bird looked down at the clutch of eggs and she was happy to see the first of her clutch breaking out of its shell. In her own way the Hen bird smiled as she watched the shell being broken open little by little. She did not interfere with this little struggle as it was a lesson to the new bird that life would not be an easy ride.

It was a fine female fledgling and the Hen bird was happy with the first of her clutch. Over time the rest of the clutch were born. All were nursed and fed and as they grew they eventually became independent and flew off to make their way in life, to continue the ebb and flow of the seagull community. Sometime later, the first of the clutch, who had been enjoying this new life, had an encounter with a fishing net and as she became ensnared, her wing was broken. The little seagull sat on the beach and stared out at the sea, wondering why she could not fly off and how long it would take for Death to claim her. As she waited, she sat and shivered, as she watched the approaching figures.

Clacton-on-Sea, that little English seaside village, just down the way from Frinton-on-Sea. Here the sands were beautiful and so was the view of the sea itself. Many people came down here for the relaxing hobby of sea fishing. One God had even made this haven his own, although he had made sure that his little haven was one second removed from the real Clacton-on-Sea (so as in a different dimension) and as such was his own Heaven. Here he could walk between Worlds. One second he could be in his own personal Heaven and the next, he could be in the real world. This was how he liked it.

It was on a glorious Monday morning that the Christ stood on the beach with his rod's handle buried in the sand as he watched the line on the end of his rod bob up and down in the sea. He watched in the hope that he might ensnare a fish at the end of his fishing line.

"This is truly Heaven," thought he.

Jesus Christ, or Chris as he liked to be known these days, stood about 6 feet tall. He appeared to be about 30 years of age. He was skinny with long-flowing black hair that reached down to his shoulders. He also had a full-face beard. He wore a denim shirt and jeans on this day, with his feet in a pair of garish yellow sandals. In short, the tall chap looked very much like a hippy. He did though have inviting eyes and a warm friendly smile. When you spoke to Chris, you always walked away with a feeling of warmth and a smile on your face.

As he fished, Chris noticed out of the corner of his eye that a small figure was approaching. This figure turned out to be a young child of around six years of age and he looked very scared.

"Hello," said the young child shyly as he neared Chris. Chris smiled warmly and radiated warmth as he looked down.

"Hello," he said in return.

"What are you doing?" asked the boy.

"Why, I am fishing, my boy," came the happy reply.

"I have lost my parents," said the little boy who then burst into tears.

Chris smiled sadly as he knew what had happened. At that moment a seagull swooped at his line and he said excitedly. "Hey, did you see that? I think we have a bite." As he said it, he grabbed a hold of the fishing rod and began trying to real in his catch.

"Help me boy, grab a hold, we must try to real this one in." The little lad was now as excited as Chris and all his worries were lost to him for a moment as he too held onto the fishing rod and the two of them began to real home the catch.

"Look at the size of it," smiled Chris.

"It's a big fish," said the little boy, smiling broadly, as they both hauled with all their combined might. As they hauled, tugged, and sweated, eventually the fish was brought onto the beach. Chris looked down at the boy and said, "Here, place your foot on its back as I bash its brains out." The small boy watched in wonder as he held down the fish with his foot and Chris bashed it on the head with a big stick. The fish stopped wriggling as the life went out of it and then Chris picked it up and smiled. "There, what do you think of that then?" he asked.

The little boy burst into tears, "You killed it! It was a beautiful fish and you killed it!"

"It was and still is a beautiful fish, young man, and it will be a beautiful supper for us. You see, God moves in mysterious ways and one of his wonders is how we must feed ourselves. This fish was sent from the Gods above so as it can be our supper. So we won't waste it and we will praise the Gods for our bounty today."

The little boy looked on in wonder and then continued to cry and asked for his parents. "My boy," Chris sought to comfort him, "your parents are both in tears about their loss too. They have lost their son and they will not see him again for some years, because he has now gone to Heaven."

"Is this Heaven then?" asked the boy.

"It is one version, and it is a happy place. We will go along to the chip shop and ask for our fish to be cooked and all the other little children will be happy to eat it."

"But I want to see my parents," said the lad.

"You can look in on them from time to time, my boy. They will not see you, although I am sure that they will feel your presence."

"It's not fair," said the little boy.

"No, it's not really, it really isn't but you will be well cared for here. And one day you will be reunited with your family."

Chris then smiled warmly at the little boy and took hold of his hand. The boy felt the warmth and love emanating from Chris's hand and they then walked together along the beach. Chris explained all the wonders that were to come and the young boy began to smile a little.

"It is quite nice here lad," said Chris, "here you will encounter all kinds of things, it can be wonderful for a boy such as yourself. Here you will meet new friends of your own age and you can have any number of adventures. You can explore caves, fly kites, ride horses and bikes, climb trees, why you can even fish if you like. This is a wonderful place and it will help you recover from your loss as you travel on your own personal journey." Chris continued talking to the boy as they walked and he seemed to brighten up a little.

As they walked somewhat further along the beach, Chris spotted a young seagull chick that was caught up in some old fishing lines.

Chris pointed it out and said, "Look at that young bird there, chap."

"It looks hurt," said the boy, "It looks as if it has a broken wing." The two of them wandered over to the bird and Chris picked it up. He studied the bird's wing and after a moment or two's fussing, he nurtured it back to where it should be.

"There," said Chris, "Everything is right again." He then placed the bird down onto the sandy beach. They both stood and watched as the seagull flew off into the sky.

"That is a small wonder to behold my boy," said Chris. He then looked down towards the small chap and smiled.

"Chips, chap?" he asked.

"Yes please," returned the boy. Chris was happy with what he had done today, what with comforting the lad and feeding the rest of the community with his fish (he had become quite adept at this over the years). He had left the boy with his new friends who were now comforting him and helping him move towards the next phase of his journey. Yes, Chris was happy and decided to take himself home to his little cottage by the sea.

This little cottage sat in both worlds, it was home to Chris both in the Heavens and on Earth; all it needed was for him to decide which place he wanted to be and at which time. While on Earth, he walked with the living but when he wished it, he could walk out of his front door and be in his own Heaven.

The Christ is a God. He can do as he pleases. If he wishes it he can walk on the sands of his chosen Heaven in Clacton-on-Sea or he can instantly cross over to the Earthly version of the place that is Clacton-on-Sea at a whim. He also lives in many other places, just slipping through the time and space barriers as he chooses.

It was a sunny day in Clacton. Holidaymakers had come from all over and were enjoying the sea and sand. Families sat on the beach and watched as their children built castles in the sand. Mothers sat wishing for fish and chip suppers and fathers thought back to when they were young and of the dreams that they had had then. Christ, or Chris as he liked to be known these days, sat on the veranda of his little cottage and stared out over the sea of the Earthly Clacton-on-Sea. "I love this World," he said to himself as he watched the waves crashing. "I think that Moses would like it here too," he thought. He sipped his tea as he read the daily newspaper. At this moment in time he was enjoying a little "Me" time and as he perused the pages, he came across a very interesting article about social networking sites on the Internet. He was very interested in social networking sites.

"In a way," he thought, "it's what I am all about. It's what life is all about really, the bringing together of people." After finishing the article and then re-reading it, Chris made a decision, "I must get myself one of these computer things." Not being a prophet to profit from the powers that he possessed so as to just create what he needed, he decided to take himself off to PC Direct (the computer shop) and buy a computer, after haggling for a good price, of course. Haggling was in his blood and he was not the sort of prophet that would not profit by accepting the first offering.

Chris walked over to his VW camper van and looked at it lovingly (could a prophet drive any other kind of vehicle?). This was what life was all about. It had the tyre on the front and it was painted with a psychedelic design; in short it was as hip as Chris. After lovingly looking at the camper van, he jumped inside and tried to start the engine. Typically the engine just would not catch and Chris had to get out of the van and then reach inside for his trusted hammer. He then laid himself underneath and began to bash the starter motor mercilessly. After the good bashing, he climbed back into the driving seat and tried again to start this little beast. He inserted the key and on the first turn, this little beast of a VW camper van roared into life.

"I love this life," shouted Chris over the noise from the engine as he drove off into the wilds of the countryside, heading towards the shop known as PC Direct. And as he drove along, he sang to himself, "Always look on the bright side of life." Life was good.

Sometime later, when he had arrived at his destination, Chris parked his VW camper van and surveyed the complex of shops in front of him. He looked long and hard at each façade and after taking a liking to PC Direct, he decided to walk straight in and talk to a shop assistant who, he hoped, could help him in his quest for knowledge. As he approached, the shop's doors made a shushing noise as they opened to each side of him. He said out aloud, "Gosh, it's just like Star Trek!" (He was of course a secret Trecky).

Chris was about to walk over to the main counter to ask for some assistance but as he looked around, he was awestruck by the many goods that were on sale.

'Gosh!' thought Chris, 'has the human race really progressed this far already? I don't believe it!'

He then walked around the shop looking at product after product, his smile getting bigger and bigger.

'This is wonderful stuff.' He looked at each and every item that he could, picking up this item and fiddling with it only to replace it so that he could try something else. He continued to try various pieces of equipment until after an hour or two he was spotted by a spotty youth who thought to himself, "Sale!"

The spotty youth then made his way over to Chris with pound signs in his eyes. 'Boy!' he thought, 'boy, am I going to make a killing.'

"Hello sir," said the spotty youth to Chris, "How can I help you?"

"Well, young chap," replied Chris, "I am really interested in one of these computer thingies."

"Ahh, you will want one of our top-of-the-range models then, so that you can play all the latest games with the best graphic card and the fastest RAM and ROM and of course a DVD writer/recorder capacity and broadband connectivity. You will also want a 26-inch monitor, flat screen of course and a printer too. You will also probably need some security and some INSURANCE."

"I don't think that I need any sheep chap, the whole RAM thing was over and done with long ago."

"I am talking about RAM, Random Access Memory. Now look here chap, you do need it and the more you have the better, you can trust me on that at least. And because you have spent so much of your hard-earned money, you will need our INSURANCE should anything go wrong with your purchase."

Chris looked at the spotty youth and said, "Listen young man, I am not used to being ripped off and I do not want your INSURANCE, all I want is a machine that can connect me to the World Wide Web. There are wonders to behold on the web and I want to be part of it."

"Well I can sell you a smaller computer if you want, but you will still want our INSURANCE."

Chris watched as a smaller offering was placed in front of him and after the spotty youth had talked him through the workings, it was agreed that he would pay a cash deal of £500 for a computer that would connect him to the World Wide Web.

Chris took out his wallet from his pocket and produced the required amount in crisp £20 notes and handed them over.

"You are £250 short there, chap," said the spotty youth.

"£500 was our agreed price," responded Chris.

"Another £250 for the INSURANCE."

"For the last time, I don't require the INSURANCE."

"You would be mad to take the computer without the INSURANCE," said the spotty youth.

"I do not want the INSURANCE, chap," said Chris.

The spotty youth was about to say some more, when Chris made some movements with his fingers and all of a sudden the spotty youth was struck speechless.

A few minutes later, Chris walked from the shop with his new computer and loaded it aboard the VW camper van.

'I can't wait to get this home and give it a try,' he told himself.

The drive home did not take too long and he soon arrived although he did not break any speed restrictions. When he had arrived, he put on the kettle and made himself a cup of tea. He then sat down to read the instructions of how to set up the computer. He plugged in all the wires and soon had the computer fired up and ready to go. He then clicked the mouse on the 'Internet' icon.

Nothing happened.

He clicked again.

Nothing.

Chris read through the instructions again and then realised his problem. This little cottage had no Internet connection.

'Hmm,' he thought, 'I shall have to get hold of the telephone company and have this problem sorted out.' And so it was that Chris went through the long process of haggling over the price with a spotty youth on the other end of the telephone line till it was agreed that an engineer would come out the very next morning to connect him to the Internet.

While he was waiting for the next morning to come, Chris walked along the beachfront and wondered at the prosperity of the people that lived in this little country. Nearly everyone was housed to some degree and no one starved any more. There were so many good Samaritans these days. There were still a few people who chose to be homeless but even these few were fed from the kindness or guilt of the people who had too much themselves.

Chris walked and walked. He was after all a God and did not need any sleep. So he walked and as he walked, travelled the land, and performed as many kindnesses as he could without being exposed to those he helped.

The man who was about to throw himself to death from the top of a tall building looked down and saw Chris smiling up at him and suddenly changed his mind. "I have found God," he was later to declare to anyone who would listen.

A man who had burgled a house saw Chris as he was leaving the scene of his crime and suddenly did not want his ill-gotten gains any more, so he broke back into the house and put the things from where he had taken them.

Two drunken revellers were fighting each other to a bloody pulp. One of them grabbed hold of a nearby house brick and was about to bash it into the head of the other fighter when he saw Chris and changed his mind. "Look!" he said and pointed towards Chris. These two fighters became firm friends from then on and although they still to this day go out drinking with each other, something has now happened to them and no matter how much alcohol they drink they cannot get drunk. They now no longer fight either.

There were many wonders that night as Chris walked the country. The rapist, who found that he could no longer gain an erection. The wife beater, who suddenly found a new degree of patience and love towards her. The man, who was embezzling little old ladies, suddenly changed overnight and started a new "free" old age people's home.

So many people change for the better when Chris walks the Earth. In the morning Chris returned home, as fresh as a daisy and smiled as he saw the engineer leaving his little cottage.

"You have finished connecting it then?" he asked.

"All done squire, you should lock your doors though, a thief could have walked in here and taken all your stuff."

"And they would be most welcome to," came the reply.

"If anyone stole from me, I would have them locked up."

"And I would forgive them."

The engineer thought to himself, 'We have a right nutter here!' and then said, "Well it's all done, enjoy yourself online, matey."

Chris smiled as the chap drove off and then walked into his little cottage. He stared at his new computer and after taking a seat he fired it up. The screen soon came to life and he clicked his mouse onto the Internet icon. A picture appeared on the screen and there was the thing he wanted right before his eyes, it said "SEARCH". Chris typed in "facebook.com" and waited. Almost instantly he was directed to the Facebook home page. He then read the instructions and followed them as he joined this social networking site. 'The World Wide Web,' he thought, 'how wonderfully strange this planet has become.'

Chris studied the Facebook home page and noticed that it wanted him to answer some basic questions.

First Name…

'Hmm,' thought he, 'Christ, of course.'

He then typed Chris.

Last Name…

'Son of God, of course.'

He thought for some time about this answer and then typed: Allove.

Your email was the next text box…

Christ@ntlworld.com, he typed.

Re-enter email…

Christ@ntlworld.com, he typed again.

Password...

Fisherman1

Sex...

Male, of course, typed Chris.

Birthday...

December 25.

He then hit the sign-up button. The web page before him was fine although it was pretty much blank. No friends yet. There was a box that indicated, "Find friends" and so he tapped in a few names just to see who had joined this website so far.

The first name he entered was "Buddy Roy". Buddy Roy was the name that his old friend The Buddha was using these days. 14 men with the name of Buddy Roy appeared on his screen. He scanned all the profile pictures and sent a friend request to his good old friend, Buddha. He then typed Shiva. Nothing! On and on he typed, looking for old friends from the past but he found nothing. At last Chris typed in "Chocolate Fudge Cabin". Instantly a picture of the ice cream house in Clacton-on-Sea appeared. "Add as Friend," asked the text box. Chris hit the yes button and was instantly sent to the "Chocolate Fudge Cabin" website. He now had his first "friend request" sent. He smiled broadly and then went on to type in as many "Friends" as he could. When he had a hundred or so requests on the way, he noticed that you could upload pictures.

"This is cool!" he thought, and then went on to upload a profile picture of himself. The picture that he uploaded showed a six-foot plus man. In the picture he looked quite young. He wore a full-face beard and smiled. You could not see his long flowing black hair because he was wearing a cowl. This cowl was part of a flowing robe that flowed down to the ground and covered all his appendages. It was in fact a classic picture of Jesus that we all know.

Some days after this picture was posted, some of his web "Friends", who had accepted his request for friendship, asked if he was at a fancy dress party when it was taken. Chris replied that it was just a natural picture but seeing that it caused a slight stir, he then posted another picture. This one showed a six-foot tall chap with very short hair who wore glasses and was clean-shaven. He was also wearing a suit and a tie.

"That's not you, is it?" asked one friend.

"It is me in my college days," came the reply.

"Something more modern would be better," commented an online friend.

Chris sat back and thought and then came up with a solution. The next picture that he posted showed a tall man in his early thirties. He sported a goatee beard. His hair was long but finely cut and rested upon his shoulders. He wore a jean jacket over a white tee-shirt which was tucked into a clean pair of blue jeans. On his feet he wore a pair of black trainers. The face itself had a hypnotic look that seemed to draw you to it. The smile seemed to have the effect of making any one who looked at it smile back.

"Great profile picture!" were the replies of many friends and soon Chris was receiving friend requests from all sorts of people that he had not heard of.

"Just like the old days!" he thought.

He was now on Facebook on a regular basis. 'I only wish that some of my old friends would get in touch. I wonder if Krishna is online and on Facebook?' he asked himself. He then typed in Kris Hna. He thought that this might well be the name that his old mate was using now; after all he had signed up using the name Chris T. Allove.

'Oh well,' he thought, 'these things take time.' He now had over a hundred mortal friends and these friends' friends were even now bombarding him with friendship requests. It was always thus. Chris had always drawn people towards him. As the days went on, Chris accepted more and more friends and he soon had over a thousand.

Then on one Thursday morning, he had a friend accepted message. Buddy Roy accepts your friendship request, click here. And click he did. There on the screen was a picture of his old friend The Buddha and as he looked, he noticed that Buddy Roy was on line at this very moment.

"Hello Buddy," typed Chris, "How are you?"

"Hello Chris, you took your time. Where have you been and where are you now?"

"I have been, and always will be, but I am living in England at the moment, a little place called Clacton, come and visit."

"Oh England, I have heard of it, it is cold and wet from what I hear. It's warm where I am and anyway I can't move at the moment as I am still perfecting levitation."

"It's nice here, best fish and chips in the world, come and try some."

"No way, they are full of fat and I can't afford to get any fatter. It's really difficult floating at the moment, as it is."

"You look well on your profile picture chap," said Chris.

"As do you, young God, have you doctored that picture, you look really young."

"Compared to you, I am young."

"That's true, oh so sorry, I must go now as Vishnu is on line and I need to talk to him, see you soon."

"Wait, can I ask, is Krishna on Facebook?"

"Of course he is, just look at my profile and you will see him, have to go now, see you." And he was gone.

Chris stared at the screen and looked at Buddy Roy's friends and there amongst the host of people that were listed as friends of Buddy Roy was Krishna.

'Good Lord, this is an exciting place!' Chris thought as he typed in the Friend request box and waited for a reply and excitement to unfold. Excitement comes at a price – who knew it better than Gods. But Chris was a modern God, he was not one to adhere to the age old proverb, 'Better be safe than sorry.'

On the other side of the world…

KRISHNA

ಬಾ

Krishna slurped, from a glass tumbler, his morning cardamom *chai* that his mother had made him before queuing up for water at the municipality tap. As far as he could recall his mother was always up and awake before the break of dawn to use the shared toilets while they were still clean. An early start to the day also ensured that her bucket was ahead in the long queue at the municipality tap, the sole fount of water for the entire population of the *chawl*. The complex or the *chawl* was a building of one-room set houses, all rented out to different families by the landlord. The one-brick wall that separated any two homes provided little privacy to the families who could hear the noises in their neighbours' homes, loud and clear. In order to keep the family secrets within the confines of their four walls, the residents had set their radio and television sets to a high volume. On some days they found themselves screaming out loud to be heard over the din of songs and news blaring from thirty radio/television sets inside the *chawl*.

The one room set, as it was referred to for the sake of differentiating between the types of accommodation available for renting, comprised a room to live and sleep in with separate areas for cooking and bathing. Within the same complex, though, one-room accommodation sans a separate bathing area was available at a lower rent.

The rooms were arranged in a U shape around the courtyard that opened out to the entrance gate of the complex. An old banyan tree stood in the middle of the courtyard, proud and green, a home to birds and monkeys, the other co-habitants of the complex. The toilets were at the end of a passage, which was an offshoot of the courtyard. The municipality tap, provided by the government, was next to the tree and therefore the tree, by virtue of its location and proximity to the one and only source of water, had come to be the hub of all activity in the *chawl*.

Water was scarce in the city of Delhi and as is with the distribution of natural resources, it was scarcer still for the poor. Yashoda's early start to the day ensured some water, even if it was half a bucket, for the family. Krishna could have saved his mother the hardships of slum life but he did not believe in crossing the realm of the real to provide for mere human wants. 'Men have to live out their destinies,' he would say to himself and participate in the daily trivia with detached amusement.

Krishna was taken up with 'human' enthusiasm as he watched the play of events at the community tap that morning. He dipped a crumbly, sweet biscuit into the milky tea before going back to enjoy the spat that was gaining crescendo with every passing minute. The subject of discussion in the *chawl* that day was Baba Somdev, who had been involved in a political controversy of late. Baba was hailed as the modern day Robinson Crusoe by some of his followers, while others called him a sham. If you were to state it in corporate parlance, Baba had started his career as a humble yoga teacher and *ayurveda* practitioner. Within a decade of starting out, he had donned the role of a public speaker with political aspirations, and had become a celebrity yoga-guru heading a business empire with a net worth of a few hundred million dollars. All through his rise to fame he had drawn flak for his ill-formed views on politics and ludicrous populist slogans, such as 'capital punishment for corruption and adultery'. However much the press ridiculed him and the politicians lampooned his public speeches, his fan-following continued to grow with gusto.

Krishna waved off the fleas that returned to the brim of his glass every few seconds and then flew back, upon being disturbed, to the morsels of last night's dinner on an infant's face. The infant's mother was a long way off from the tap. Just like other women lined up in the queue, she was not interested in Baba Somdev, nor did she have any view on adultery or corruption. All she wanted, at that moment, was to secure her child inside the room, away from the fleas, and fill as many buckets as she could with precious water. All these excitable men, who were engrossed whole-heartedly in the debate on Baba, were far removed from Baba and his enemies. These men, now in the throes of passion over Baba's ideals, had not the remotest access to the power corridors of their country. They had to wait their turn at the tap, and to their minds there was nothing as grand as national politics. Participating in such debates these men felt less insignificant than they were. They barely eked out a living for themselves and their big families and had so very little to live by that they chose not to look at the grimness that surrounded their lives. Also, because they had nothing to hold on to, they loved, argued, and prayed with such fervour that Krishna was impelled to join them in his last incarnation. Where else was life so buoyant and precariously deficient?

Krishna has chosen to live in a slum close to the opulent South Delhi. He has returned so as not to let down his devotees who have awaited his incarnation. They wait for him because in the oral tradition that has come to them over the centuries, it is said that Krishna shall return in the *Kalyuga*. In his present incarnation, Krishna lives incognito with his mother who, some say, was a prostitute in her youth. Far too many stories have been invented over the years about his mother's past. Once every few years a malicious story is exhumed by someone in the neighbourhood to keep the gossip alive. It's another matter that no one cares for truth any more.

In Delhi a slum is never too far from the rich neighbourhoods and however much the rich roll up the windows of their cars, the poor come knocking at them as a reminder that they too inhabit the city. Slums are illegal and un-authorized colonies that can be neither regularized nor bulldozed. They are unplanned clusters of houses and commercial complexes without any legal sanction and therefore are not entitled to any civic amenity – not even water. Therefore, the poor steal what is not lawfully theirs. Open sewers, uncovered drainage manholes, and overflowing drains are accepted as a given in life. It is no small wonder that Krishna chose the most marginalized of all for his *sakhas*. A lusty brown lad, with eyes so deep and mirthful, Krishna goes about life gaily, with optimism of youth and joy of hope. He surges to seek life in a city that the town planners fear is on the brink of a collapse.

Children of the poor are expected to supplement their household income even before they can learn to count on their fingers. Krishna's first job with a *halwai* had required him to report at seven in the morning and work till ten at night for a pittance of remuneration. His work profile included everything from mopping the floors, to cleaning the tables, to emptying garbage into an MCD bin close by, to carrying hot trays of set *burfi* – just about everything they could use him for, even massaging the *halwai's* thick shoulders. At the age of seven, when he had started out his work life, Krishna was required to be on the job 15 hours a day, all seven days of the week, for a mere Rs.2,000 a month.

Since he was God, he managed; not that a human child had any choice. Krishna had quickly, through his growing years, learnt something of many trades. By the time he reached pubescence, Krishna had acquired quite a few skills. He had served as an apprentice to the tailor, the grocer, the shoe-maker, the bus conductor besides working at a carton-making factory, a school canteen, and even the hazardous fire-crackers' making unit; nothing Godly about that. Nowadays, 16-year-old Krishna works as a pantry boy in a 300-bed private hospital @ Rs.100 a day. The minimum age of employment as set by the labour laws is 18 years, but laws are rarely heeded in this land of *dharma*.

SUNDERAMAN

ॐ

Mr. Sunderaman, the store manager at the dietetics department in the hospital that Krishna works in, draws two per cent kickbacks of the wages of all contractual employees. The hospital management has of late been following the policy of hiring contractual workers rather than employing a permanent workforce. At one time the labour union of the hospital employees had become a threat to the management, holding the authorities and patients to ransom. To counter the growing menace of the labour union, the management laid off the old permanent workers on some excuse or the other and the working of some departments was outsourced to contractors. The likes of Sunderaman, who had pledged allegiance to the management, made a killing while the oppressive class and the oppressed labour settled their differences.

Sunderaman had joined the hospital's laundry department at the age of 20 as an apprentice to Mr. Roy, the laundry manager. At 25, he developed asthma from working long hours in the laundry. It was not uncommon for young men to suffer from respiratory diseases because of prolonged exposure to steam and damp surroundings. Sunderaman was then moved to the store in the dietetics department where he regained his health and with time also came to yield power over his juniors. At 45, he may not have progressed significantly in his career or salary, but he has generated wealth by other means. All supplies that come into the dietetics department bring him some favour in cash or kind. Some suppliers provide rations for his home directly at his doorstep, while others oblige him with gifts on Diwali and New Year.

Krishna, with his pleasant, clever ways, is his favourite pantry boy. But when it comes to his pound of flesh, Sunderaman does not differentiate between a favourite and a non-favourite. Krishna is one boy who happily runs errands, posts Sunderaman with cricket scores, and tips him off on nurses. Sunderaman was particularly happy with the tip-off that day; Sister Shiny was on evening shift! Shiny was a 23-year-old, pleasant looking, voluptuous nurse from his hometown, Alpe. Sunderaman was polishing off his morning *parantha* when Krishna returned with cricket news.

"Sir, a bad day for India! We are four wickets down, Tendulkar's gone."

"Bastards! None of them know how to play cricket, bunch of sister f*****s, that's what they all are! And Tendulkar is getting old. They ought to retire him. Have you set the trolley of the 3rd A ward, Krishna? Don't tell me you haven't done it yet! You're getting slack Krishna, that won't work with me! I'm good but I can be a mean bastard if I want to be." Sunderaman was used to barking orders at the pantry boys all day long, without moving an inch in his office chair that barely accommodated his girth.

"Don't say that Sir, I went to the doctors' room for your sake. Did you not ask me to post you with an hourly cricket update? I am the only one who runs around for your personal updates about nurses and all that, and yet you complain about me! Now look at Kanhiya, he has not done my trolley yet. He washes my trolley last of all."

"Send Kanhiya over here! Bastards all of them! All they want is to sit on their arses and fill their stomachs!"

"No point Sir, he will not come in. You will have to go and catch him in the mess. The boys are at a game of cards over there. But mind you Sir, if someone discovers this tip-off business, I'll lose my job. Be careful lest I land in trouble. My word, the new Sister-in-charge is a tough spinster. You can't fool her! No one dare mess with the girls in her ward."

Sunderaman was not one to be manipulated, but with Krishna he found himself floundering, and there was Sister Shiny to catch; a nubile bud he was infatuated with. Once Krishna left his office, Sunderaman picked up his huge form from the chair, hurling expletives at the whole world, Tendulkar included.

"You sister f*****, come here," he yelled out, standing in the middle of the kitchen area, to the group of boys at a game of cards. The group being addressed was a motley mix of young boys and middle-aged men who were referred to by a generic name – pantry boys. They were called thus because they belonged in the pantries attached to the wards.

"Which one do you want?" someone yelled back.

The room shook with laughter. The boys were amused at the repartee directed against the voice of authority.

"You bastards, don't shoot at me from there, come here and face me like a man, mother-f*****s, all of you. Even women have more courage than all you men put together. Go on, laugh like eunuchs do! Why don't you also clap your hands and dance like them?" Sunderaman clapped loud and thrust his pelvis forward to emphasize his manhood. The boys gave themselves over to another frenzy of laughter. They were more amused than offended by his obscene gesture.

"I say stop it! You're back to your old ways, Sunderaman! This is a department, not a fish market for you to stand and hurl abuses," Mrs. Desai screamed from behind Sunderaman's back. Sunderaman was caught off-guard. He had not seen his boss emerge out of her office and watch his 'eunuch dance'. By now the laughter in the cards room reached a mad crescendo.

"I want you in my office, now! And you had better have a good explanation, Sunderaman, because only last week you swore upon your daughter to never use cuss words, ever! Have some shame man, you have a grown-up girl at home!" Mrs. Desai, the chief of the dietetics department, glowered at the boys, who were hushing themselves to silence, knowing that they had once again broken the decorum of the workplace.

Krishna returned from the ward after an hour since Sunderaman had been reprimanded in full public view. Since he was God he knew what had transpired while he was away to the ward, but as a man he had to feign ignorance.

"Here, today's paper, crisp and fresh. It's not easy to sneak it out from patients' rooms, these days. You are lucky, 306 died this morning. Poor guy; was in his forties. Had he been 70-something, you wouldn't have even got the headlines. Ha, ha," Krishna laughed at his own joke.

On some days he felt he was beginning to sound human. Was it his love for mankind that made him slip into human skin with such ease; or was it his revulsion to decline in human values that caused him to return to the *Indralok*? He was never sure.

"Shut up you bastard! Caw, caw, caw! You go cawing all day long! Ever asked your mother if she had you with a crow? Get out of my office! It's entirely my fault; I treated the likes of you at par and you have become monsters! My father always said, 'Sunderaman, my son, do not talk to guys lower down. Keep them in their place and they will respect you! Mind you, pat a dog and he bites you, kick him and he licks your toes! Such is human nature, my son!'"

Sunderaman spat on the floor. He paused to admire the bubbles form and burst on the surface of the rich, frothy saliva. He looked for signs of disgust on Krishna's face but Krishna remained silent and impassive.

"Keep off me Krishna, I am bloody angry — *huh*. Go tell those mother f*****s that I will teach them a lesson soon; remember to tell them it will be soon. And you Krishna, you never tell me what's going on amongst you boys. Don't forget, I gave you this job. Never bite the hand that feeds you, you wretched ungrateful dog. Beware, if I change my mind about you, you will be on the streets again. Stay in your place, you petty servant!"

Sunderaman tilted his head to one side to see the effect of his expletives. With him, his huge stomach moved to the left, and then jerked to the right after hitting the corner of the table. After shifting about for a minute, the huge mass of flesh settled around its axis.

A tall boy with broad shoulders, Krishna towered well above this burly officer who sat across the table. Sunderaman picked up the newspaper that Krishna had placed on the table. He skimmed through a few pages, searching for gossip and flipped to page three. Soon he was shaking again, his body in tandem with his mood as he laughed. He laughed heartily, now that he was in the grip of mirth. The chair creaked in protest all over again. He was one of those men who easily gave themselves over to emotion, and once in its grip they submitted to it wholly.

"*Eh* Krishna, come, read this feature; it's about Facebook. This world of computers is very advanced, my boy! While you and I live a life of drudgery, this world has real fun. You imbecile boy, do you know anything about computers, at all? *Huh*, don't look baffled you illiterate fool – go, learn some primary school stuff."

Krishna smiled at a visibly pleased Sunderaman; he, the God, smiled because this man who bullied others was ignorant of the humiliation that life was due to return him. Krishna smiled because Sunderaman did not know that the excitement he sought from cricket and newspapers was a compensation for the emptiness in his life. He smiled, as Gods tend to, at man's smugness.

"Are you not on Facebook, Sir?" Krishna looked directly at his senior. Sunderaman found Krishna's gaze disconcertingly direct and probing.

"Why do you stare at everybody, you bastard? Now instead of chatting up people, read the newspapers, you will be better informed that way. Look there is so much here," he thrust the paper in Krishna's face, "Read, ha ha, but you can't read, you sister f*****, you can't read, can you?"

Krishna merely smiled at the abuses hurled at him. He heard them out as if they were mere words. After Sunderaman had finished talking, Krishna composed a calm reply, "I can read very well, I learnt at an evening school, Mr Sunderaman. The truth, Sir Sunderaman, is that I pass on the paper to you after I've scraped every bit of the information myself. I have read this one, and yes, I am on Facebook, I just don't find time from work to be active on social media." Krishna walked away, graceful like a peacock, head high and shoulders square beneath a proud neck.

Sunderaman's jaw dropped at Krishna's words, but he quickly collected his wits about him and shouted behind his back, "You scourge of the brothel! How dare you! Dare enter my room again, you sister f*****!" Retreating in his steps, Krishna stopped to cast a glance of disapproval. For reasons unknown to him, Sunderaman, the boor, felt a chill run down his spine.

THE FRIEND REQUEST

෨

It was late in the evening. The visitors who came to see the patients were shooed away by the guards, after the visiting hours had passed, bringing back some semblance to the cardiac ward. Krishna sat in front of a computer with a Wi-Fi connection provided for the resident doctors in the doctors' rest room. From the window, across the road, he could see the backyard of a church; now a gloomy grey in twilight. Krishna tended to grow pensive at this hour of day. What if Christ was, like him, searching for his own echo somewhere? What if he, too, had taken a new *avatar*? And what if he had never left? It was a choice only Gods were given; to never grow old and to continue living for as long as they thought was necessary. Further, he reflected on his own state of being, on the *karambhoomi* that he had chosen for himself; a hospital in the third world, so as to be by the side of men on their deathbed. He, the Almighty, had taken it upon himself to ease the departure of dying men and women, making their transit to the other world more peaceful. He held the shriveled, diseased bodies in his strong arms, feeling their nervous hearts in his palm as he eased their pain with a smile. These men on the verge of death found comforting reassurance in the dancing eyes of this pantry boy. Krishna, the God, embraced them without inching one step in their direction. He smiled at them, radiating joy like the rainbow in the sky. They in turn, smiled back, forgetting their pain and impending fate.

"Okay world! Here we go," Krishna spoke aloud as the computer screen threw up his log-in name. In a second he took his virtual *avatar*. On his Facebook 'wall' opened the list of all 2,480 friends, five messages, 30 notifications, and a new friend request.

Not one of his friends was known to him in real life. Krishna had cooked up a fictitious identity of a 33-year-old bachelor, Krish, a resident of Mumbai. Krish was a struggling artist on Facebook. He had uploaded his artwork for display on his wall. "Your paintings have an emotive force which is both unique and powerful," was another artist's comment on his work. To Krishna, his virtual identity was as fictitious as the identity he had taken on in this world.

"After all, we are all trying to pass off as something in this world. Who is the real artist? Who is the real God? Maybe the artist is a salesman and the beggar is the artist!" he would debate with his virtual friends. He got down to replying to messages from lovelorn women; and then he wrote a quote on his wall, citing the Gita as source. Of late, however, he was beginning to tire of virtual connections, mostly because most women wanted him to profess love, which he did not feel. Being a God he could neither lie nor mislead; a sin he knew men committed without any compunction. So he switched off his chat and pondered over his Facebook wall. He scrolled down his friends' list, going over their smiling photographs. They were there and not quite there in his world. 'Will I ever connect with human beings the way they do with each other?' He was beginning to feel lonesome in the virtual world.

In order to gain small favours, like using the Internet, Krishna played the 'Robin Hood'; sneaking from the coffers of the rich to feed the employees and the poor patients. On his evening shift Krishna pilfered meals for the doctor-on-duty to gain access to the computer and Internet. It is another thing that the food, the computer, and the Internet connection belonged neither to Krishna nor any doctor. They were, in fact, the personal property of a multimillionaire industrialist. The hospital was a profit-making business entity for the owner who had invested in all sorts of business ventures. Of late the pilferage of supplies, wastage, doing social media during duty hours, and the employees' lackadaisical attitude at work was eating into the profits of the hospital. Krishna and other employees justified their action as reverse justice. Reverse justice, as an idea, had been mooted to undo God's wrongs – a kind of socialist drive against the Gods.

'How boring it is these days, what wouldn't I give for a warm, intelligent conversation,' Krishna murmured under his breath. 'Now Buddy Roy is a good chat, but he is a bit dry. Is there no human friend who can warm the cockles of my heart, at the moment? Am I getting lonely?'

He shifted his gaze from the computer screen to the window on his left, and drew a deep breath. The church was a dark outline against the night sky. The cross stood proud in the faint moonlight, gleaming like a warrior's sword.

"Hey you! What do you think you are doing here?" a young resident doctor with a thick black moustache stood at the door, scowling at Krishna. His pitch was shrill and overly loud, perhaps to make up for the lack of inches in his height. Krishna had grown accustomed to the doctors' brusque treatment of him and other junior staff. The doctors thought themselves more important because they had coveted degrees which translated into fat salaries and a higher status in the social hierarchy. They were blind to the truth that they were, like every other employee, mere cogs in the wheel – one no more indispensable than the other.

"Easy, he's Krishna, he works around here," Dr Amarjeet, a happy-go-lucky, hirsute, young Sikh doctor came from behind his colleague to Krishna's aid. He placed his hand on Krishna's shoulder, squeezing it in warm affirmation and gratitude for all the meals he had been fed from the pantry. The new resident doctor looked on in disbelief at the display of affection by a doctor towards a man of common existence.

"Have you not had food from his pantry yet? No? Krishna, what's this, boy, you haven't welcomed doctor sahib! Go fetch him something to eat. By the way, what do you have for dessert today?" Dr Amarjeet was pleased at the bargain he had got himself. In anticipation of eating some delectable pudding the insouciant doctor squeezed his colleague's shoulder with effusive camaraderie. The gesture had an opposite effect on the newly recruited doctor, who felt slighted at being treated at par with a man of a lower descent. He shrank in disgust and looked about uneasily. 'This greedy Amarjeet can stoop so low for mere food,' he thought to himself.

Krishna served the food that had been stocked for a late night admission. It was not uncommon for a sick man, in need of immediate medical attention, to be hauled by traffic on the roads and what with the interminably tedious admission procedure the newly-admitted patients were bound to feel hungry upon arrival. Therefore all pantries were stocked with some extra food for the night. Fed and placated, the young petulant doctor left for the wards and Krishna returned to the computer.

'Hell! I just hope no hungry patient turns up tonight!' Krishna thought to himself as the Windows operating system appeared on the computer screen and then connected to the Wi-Fi connection of the hospital. He was never happy about putting to use his Godly intervention for every little problem like using the Internet and the feeding of hungry patients. 'I suppose I will have to sneak rations from Sunderaman's stock,' Krishna chuckled at the thought of Sunderaman.

He quickly logged into his Facebook account to check out the new friend request that awaited him. He was curious about the new request which he had not been able to look up because his last browsing session had been suddenly interrupted. And now as he studied the profile picture and the information provided by the fellow requesting virtual friendship, a feeling of déjà vu grew.

'Is it who I think it is?' The lean, handsome Englishman who wore a goatee beard and a charming smile looked God-like and handsome. As is with Gods, he had more women than men on his Friends list.

'It has to be you buddy—uumn, let us check your whereabouts? Clacton-on-Sea, England. Yay!' Chris had beaten him to it. Krishna was elated to be reunited with his friend from past lives. His long fingers danced on the keyboard as he thought of all the things that he had always wanted to share with this friend who matched him perfectly in mind and spirit. He typed a personal message along with accepting the request. Every now and then as he looked at the screen, his eyes twinkled with mischief and he said to himself, 'So we meet again, my friend.'

The message read:

Hello Chris, my brother. How are you? So you pipped me to the post! I wanted to get to you first, not that we need modern-day connections to talk. But am I not glad that you found me! I was not certain about your whereabouts. Tell me how is Clacton for a home? As you know I live in the city of Delhi. It is a strange city, my friend. The rich live off the poor here. In times of economic boom the rich grow richer and in times of recession the poor become poorer. It's an ominous city which feeds on its poor to flourish. I must admit that this city makes me feel less Godly! At times I think I am beginning to lose myself in the daily trivia. Life catches you here and you end up participating more than you wanted to. I am beginning to miss the company of Gods. Now isn't it great that the very man we created has devised a means to network us. Wink! I like to say to my God friends in heavens, "Man can be downright petty and adorably silly." But now that we are here my friend, let us put the earthly devices to good use. xxx

The world turned a little...

Clacton-on-Sea...

It had been some days now since Chris had sent out his invite for a friend invitation via Facebook to Krishna. Time moved on, as it tended to, and as it moved, Chris waited. He was not idle in his waiting though and, as he waited, he made plans. He was planning a big surprise for his old friend Krishna. 'It is your birthday soon, chap,' thought Chris, 'and what we need is a beach barbeque with some music and dancing. Boy, is this going to be some party, all we need is some of the old Gods and it will be party on.'

The world turned, of course, it always did. Come Man or God, the World always turned.

A LOVE STORY

∞

On Earth, a death was imminent. It was approaching in a hospital in London. The man had been suffering for some time and as he faced his final hours, his wife squeezed his hand so as to give him the courage that she thought he would need to face the afterlife that was approaching.

"We had a good life, my love," she said as she squeezed his hand.

"I will always love you, you know my dear, even when I am dead. Then I will love you from the other side."

"I know that you will, my love, and I will always love you too. Every breath I take, I will think of you."

"You know, my love, you are still young and I would hate to think of you alone for the rest of your life, when I am gone. I would hope that you take another lover and live out your final days with him."

"I will never take another, my love, I couldn't."

"You should though; it is a shame that you should have to stay alone in this life. I will wait for you in the afterlife but don't be as lonely as I am as I wait for you."

"You must rest, my dear, what will be will be, both in this life and the next."

As these two old lovers crushed each other's hands with their love, one of them died and sauntered off to heaven.

In Heavenly Clacton-on-Sea, Chris stood at the bar of the local public house as the man appeared. "Where am I?" asked he.

"Why, this is Clacton-on-Sea," said Chris with a smile.

"I was in hospital only a moment ago," said the man.

"And now you are in Clacton-on-Sea," came the reply from Chris, "how do you feel?"

"Hungry, I could eat a horse."

"We have fish, we eat a lot of it here, this being the seaside."

"Will I see my wife again?" asked the man, who had now realized what had happened to him.

"Oh surely, one day, but for now let me introduce you to some of the others." Christ always liked to welcome all the newcomers personally as often as he could. It was a way of getting everyone together.

Back on Earth, the man's wife mourned for a few years. But time is a thief. It can rob you of your senses if you are not careful and after reviewing the situation, the man's wife met another man and these two became lovers. This relationship spanned some 20 years until this pair of lovers was involved in a plane crash. Both were killed instantly and now sat on the beach at the heavenly Clacton-on-Sea.

'Oh well,' thought Chris as he walked to meet them, 'this should be interesting.'

"Hello you two and welcome to Clacton-on-Sea."

"I can honestly say chap that this is not the holiday destination that we were aiming for," said the man with a grin.

"No, I am sure that it was not," said Chris with a friendly, knowing smile.

Both new arrivals looked at the man before them and instantly realized where they were.

"Heaven then?" asked the woman.

"One version," came the reply.

"Is my first love here?" asked the woman with an anxious look.

"Oh yes, he is here," came the reply.

"Will I meet him?" asked the woman, not with fear but with interest.

"It is welcome night at the Swan Inn tonight and I believe that it is your old lovers' night to be behind the bar, serving the drinks."

"But I have a new love, what will he think?"

"Perhaps you should ask him and, of course, his new love also."

"He has a new love?" asked the old love.

"Eternity is a long time and time moves on and love flows forever in its own way."

"He won't be angry then?"

"Anger is not allowed in Clacton-on-Sea, are you angry?"

The woman smiled.

Christ smiled back, "Go and make yourselves comfortable." And he pointed to a beach hut that had been designated for them. "That is your new home, when you have freshened up, go and make yourselves known to the community at the Swan Inn."

These two newcomers wandered off and Chris smiled to himself as he faded back to the Earth that we know.

Life goes on, of course, and Chris appeared once again on the beach on Earth and walked off towards his cottage by the sea. He was happy as he walked into his beach hut and went straight to the kettle for a hot cup of tea. Chris really enjoyed this simple process. He loved the smell of the fresh tea leaves and he would sometimes smell them in his hands before rolling them gently and then dropping them into the teapot. He would then add the boiling water and wait for the tea to brew nicely. He never added milk or sugar, as he loved the taste of the tea alone.

Chris sat before his computer and placed his tea upon the table beside him. He then fired up the computer and after logging into Facebook looked at the message that had been left for him by Krishna. Chris's face smiled broadly, at last his true friend had replied. As he read the message from Krishna, Chris's smile grew bigger and bigger. 'So you still have your old charm then,' he thought. 'You still just probe for answers in your own inimitable way and you still make me smile.' Chris looked at the computer screen in front of him. He then stretched out his clasped hands before himself and cracked his knuckles. "Ouch," said he, "I must stop doing that." Chris rubbed his fingers and smiled as he remembered how he had picked up this particular habit. 1970s', TV really was such a pain, that's why he had stopped watching the wrestling.

'Oh well,' he thought, 'here goes.' Chris started to type:

Hello brother, It seems that I did pip you at the post as is said in England, but who knows. How long have you been using this new fantastic tool that they call the Internet? For me, I have only just started and it quite amazes me at how ingenious these mortals can be. I wanted to contact you by this method because I am tired of using my God-like powers. We should try to live with these mortals to understand them and what better way, if not to use the same methods that they are using. I hope that you are well, brother. As for me, I am settled now, I live amongst the mortals in this little place called Clacton-on-Sea and I love it. I love it here so much that I have created my own version in the heavens and this is where I welcome the newly passed-on souls that have departed from the Earth. It is a fine place and I hope that you will come and visit me here soon. In fact if Delhi is upsetting you, then why not come and stay for a while. It will be your birthday soon. I wish to arrange a party in your honour, brother. You could stay for a few days anyway. As for the trivia of the daily grind, it gets to me sometimes too. You just have to get on with it. I find that fishing helps. I could lend you one of my rods, you would love the fishing here. The living do indeed have a funny way of making you care too much. Come and stay, I have invited Buddy Roy and the Little old Man, they are great beings to be around and they really do take your mind off reality for a second or two. As for the pettiness of mankind, it makes me smile sometimes; it really cannot be allowed to jade your mind too much. When you arrive here, we can reminisce about the times that we had as children.

I was just thinking the other day about the adventures that we had when we were kids.

I am lonely, being a God is so intense. Yes it is enjoyable, yes it is challenging. But who do we have to share our joys and our problems with? Yes I am lonely, but you know that. I do miss you, I searched with the help of this computer for some time but you had hidden yourself well. It took an age to find you. Are you safe where you are?

As I have said, it is a long time since we got together and I must say that I have missed you. Clacton-on-Sea is a wonderful place. As I said to Buddy Roy, they have the best fish and chips here. I am still walking my patch and performing as many miracles as I can on a daily basis. But how I would like some company. Some God-like company at that; the company of someone who walks the same path as me. Which brings me to the reason, or one of them, for approaching you. I am planning a beach party. We can invite anyone we like and party on the beach for a day or two. I have had a word with Jimmy Hendrix and he has said that he is prepared to give a song or two. I was wondering if you could have a word with George Harrison, as he is one of yours now and see if he is prepared to sing a song or two. This could be the ultimate charity gig where we all donate a miracle or two to a good cause. I will be on line on Monday from 1900 onwards. Could we get together and discuss this, matey? Let me know. God, I miss you.

JOANA

બ

"Good evening *Chechi*," Krishna winked at the middle-aged Sister-in-charge of the paediatric ward.

"What's the trouble with your left eye, boy, it is forever on the blink? You are too young for all this Krishna, and even though I may not look it, I am your mother's age. Save the eye for another time, my boy." Sister Joana was a spinster to the world. But to her own mind and in the recesses of her heart, she was still young and appealing. She lamented to her friends that but for the silly pinafore apron and the nurse's coiffeur, which she wore as part of a nurse's uniform, she would have had many doctors for admirers. The cap stood on her plump face like a hen's plume, accentuating her flaws and giving her a comical appearance. Krishna knew a woman's heart like no man could ever know. It is no small wonder that he had been a *sakha* to all the young women of Brindavan. He felt for Joana's acute loneliness. His wistful smile that skimmed her face now touched the core of her pain.

"You still look young and appealing, Sister Joana; more so when you wear those long flowing skirts in after-duty hours. Nowadays hospitals are stylizing nurses' uniforms, but our *lalaji* is an old-timer, too bad for young girls like you."

Krishna handed her tea in a disposable cup, moving about with grace and chivalry that comes to a seasoned lover (was he not a prolific lover himself?)

'His demeanour and pride are unbecoming of a worker,' thought Joana.

34

"Shut up, you naughty boy! Who are you trying to impress, are you after one of my girls?"

Joana's defences and firm veneer dropped in Krishna's presence. With him she felt lighter in her soul, which was weary of loving men who had deserted her at some point or the other. Her eyes sparkled at his words of admiration though she knew they were outrageously exaggerated lies.

"Who, me? Oh no, I prefer older women. (Winks) I have a titbit for you Sister, but first you must promise not to divulge this secret in even the most tempting of gossip sessions."

"Krishna, I don't trust you one bit, my boy. So run along and here throw this cup in the bin for me, kid. I am busy."

"You don't believe me Sister Joana; I swear upon my father, even though I don't know his name, but I am sure he lives on somewhere. All these men who produce bastards like me don't die young. They must live long to have enlarged prostrates and suffer incontinence. It's the comeuppance meted out by the Universe, *Chechi*."

"Krishna, my boy, you have such juvenile notions about the divine, did you read the Holy Bible I gave you the other day? I can understand why you have not found answers to your sorrows in your faith. Come and visit the priest in our parish, my child. You will understand then that there is only one Father, and that we must forgive others because He forgives our sins."

"*Chechi*, you know what, you cannot proselytize me. I know Christ better than any living Christian. Don't mind, *Chechi*, but missionaries are regular visitors to our slum; let's say we have a mass at our doorstep. You see we were stuffed up to here with Indian sweets," Krishna pointed to his throat and Joana found this affront to Christ in bad taste. "Besides missionaries, all election contestants gave us chocolates to sit through their speeches, I tell you, our saviours - the evangelizing missionaries and the power-yielding politicians, haha! They are the only ones who give us wages without labour." Krishna's eyes danced with mischief as his body laughed in tandem with his heart. Joana could not bear others' happiness any more than she could bear her loneliness.

"Get lost, you sinner! All that you will ever be is a menial servant. You insult others, you, who are not worth a dime. No wonder you were born a bastard!" Sister Joana turned to leave the nursing station where she had been taking notes. Krishna smiled at the mention of the word that had come to be his label in this world. He thought of his mother's eyes that had turned sad after years of humiliation. He thought of the courage she had summoned to give birth to him in adversity although she had the option of aborting the foetus. And then raising him in spite of dire resources where a lesser woman would have deserted a child; women such as her were the *Kalis* of *Kalyuga*.

"And I do hope Sister Joana that you will not die a spinster." Krishna walked away without stopping to hear Joana's vituperative outburst.

Krishna sat, that evening, in front of the computer thinking of Joana and his own mother; the two women betrayed in love, one way or the other they had been wronged. Men are born to suffer and bring suffering unto each other; he was not sure if Gods had willed it that way. It was a difficult night ahead; at least five patients were breathing their last; they had battled hard through their life and now they were ready to depart.

'Time to relieve you, my dears,' he was given to say.

'Fine, let's see what Chris has to say,' he smiled at the new distraction and unwittingly looked out of the window to the church across the street.

Log in – Password – Messages – and there it was, happily teasing him into another world. He knew he had to answer it rightaway because it was going to be a busy and eventful night for him. He typed the reply in the message box:

Chris, buddy, you look your happy-hippy self on the Facebook. So what can I tell you? You are my *sakha* from afore lives and we have been together since God knows when. You were always ambitious to venture out on your own, my younger brother! Therefore you found another religion – I am happy for you.

So you live on an island! My dearest friend, I am in the middle of an ocean, swarming with people.

However much I try, I cannot leave this country. I did think of going west, but Brindavan beckoned me. Even Gods can't escape their destiny – can we? I try not to return, but then I can't choose that either.

I am glad men have made advances such as networks and robotics, but don't you see, my friend, here lies the beginning of their end – mankind's end. And then you and I will create another sun, another moon, and another set of creatures! Oh! What wouldn't I give to make another species that can love like men do!

Don't worry about my security, friend. I am under no threat, at least not any serious threat. But you know how desperate things can get in the Third World. If they were to find out that I am who I am, they would lynch me. They do not understand that it is not I who has brought them woes. But if we were them, we would have revolted as well; what say you?

I have returned over *yugas* because of their *bhakti* – their unflinching faith and love; I go away because they refuse to follow my path. Are you not disappointed in mankind, the way they are disappointed in us? Their insatiable greed and lust makes me sick, I am truly disappointed, my friend! But maybe you don't mind, after all your following has swelled. You have done well in winning people over to your faith, yes, I must give it to you. What I ask of you is that has mankind evolved any further with new religions? Are these 'converted' men and women any more evolved than they were before? Game of numbers and power, my friend, that's all there is to it.

Maybe we could all do with that beach party; Buddy Roy has been rather melancholic of late. Vishnu loves networking, lol. Let's drop our sacks of burden for a while, and float in merriment as only

Gods can. You decide the menu, and don't forget, some of us are vegetarians over here. Oh you guys can never party without dance, can you? This fixation with the kinesis of the physical body, should we not rather leave it to human beings? But then let me not spoil the show. Go Chris; do it your way. I will be there, I promise.

Just then, Antonio's wife, Stephanie, peeped into the doctors' room in her moment of desperate search.

"Krishna! Is that you? Fancy you working on a computer! Huh, anyway, have you seen Dr Rawat? Antonio is in terrible pain, I don't know what went wrong at dialysis today? Oh dear! I wish we could help him."

Krishna promptly logged off and swiftly got to his feet, covering the distance with his long, muscular legs and surged to the door.

"You go to the room and see to *Saheb,* madam, I will fetch the resident doctor-on-duty. I will be back in a jiffy," he went past her. Stephanie knew Krishna was a saviour of sorts. He managed small miracles with a smile.

At about midnight Krishna turned up again in the room with a cup of tea. Stephanie had fallen asleep on the chair by her husband's bedside. Antonio had been on dialysis for seven years now. She looked into Krishna's eyes shining in the dark like stars on a cloudy night, all-knowing and sympathetic.

"Here madam, I made some tea for the nursing staff, why don't you have some." He seemed in no hurry to leave. Stephanie felt he was there for a reason.

"Thanks Krishna, you are God's own angel in this hospital. Come, let's go out to the corridor, Antonio is bad tonight – I just hope…" she stopped short and looked at Antonio's pinched face. She eased a crease on his forehead with her fingers, waking him up one last time.

"You will manage without me, Stephie, won't you? Oh! My stomach, its pancreatitis, isn't it? So we have reached the last stage!"

She sobbed helplessly whenever he spoke of the inevitable.

"Shh, keep still dear, you will feel better with sunrise. They have started a new dose of antibiotics for pancreas; it's not set in yet. And your kidneys are doing fine with dialysis, and now even your haemoglobin's picked up – oh! Let's not talk about this now, sleep darling, just one night of pain and you will be fine. Krishna's made me some tea, I will be back soon. You try and get some sleep, dear; I promise you a better morning."

"God bless that boy; he has been for us more than the doctors. This world is not such a bad place after all. Go then." He shut his eyes and she watched the lines of pain return to his face.

Krishna passed the cup without speaking a word. She followed him into the pantry with a strange premonition in her heart.

"He's not well tonight, I fear the worst, but I have been praying hard, and then there are the kids," Stephanie chattered on nervously. Krishna watched her in silence.

"Why do you make him suffer, hasn't he been through enough pain already, is seven years not a long time? Look there behind you, look at that cross – don't you believe in Him, your God? Will He not provide for your children? Release him, let your husband go now, trust your lord if you don't believe me." Stephanie followed his finger that pointed in the direction of the church and felt a calm grow on her.

Antonio died later that night, peaceful in the thought that Christ had appeared to him in his sleep. There was a faint smile on his face, thought Stephanie.

'I know it's you Lord, I can feel it, but why do you look like Krishna, silly me." That is how Antonio left this world, laughing at his own dream.

Monday...

1900...

Chris sat before his computer and wondered at the things that were to become. He had been sitting there for 15 minutes and had meditated so as to calm his inner self. He so wanted to talk to Krishna and now the scene was set... and as he sat and thought...

CASUALTY OF WAR

൰

S he stands on the banks of the river…
Not knowing whether to jump or not…
  She looks into the water and sees her reflection…
  A reflection that ripples and distorts…
  It is a good reflection.
  'Should I jump?' she asks herself.
  Two years together…
  Two long years…
  And only six months of real happiness…
  The rest…
  Something to rely on…
  A happy zone supposedly…
  A comfort zone definitely.
  'Should I jump?' The thought keeps coming and going, getting
more intense each time.
  Their arguments had been going on for some time now but there
always seemed to be a get-it-out-of-the-mind clause, a way back, a
way back to the comfort zone. This time, but this time the words hurt
like never before.
  'Should I jump?' she asked herself again.
  In a way the water looked clean…
  Clean enough to wash away the hurt…
  Clean enough to wash away the memories…
  Clean enough to…
  'Should I jump?'

'I loved him so much,' she kept repeating to herself, 'and I know he loved me at one point.'

'Should I jump?'

'Where is he now?' she asked herself, 'does he care where I am?'

'Probably with that floozy, he doesn't care about me.'

'Should I jump?'

She looked at the water one last time…

SPLASHHHHHHHHHHHHH…

…SPLASHHHHHHHHHHHHHH.

ARRIVAL

୫୬

Chris was just about to log on when he received that spark in his head. The spark that informed him that a life had just gone. The spark that had been life. That life spark had just dimmed! And then as it arrived, it sparked again and shone as bright if not brighter than before.

He looked at the computer console and smiled, he had been about to contact his old friend but now this. Always something. 'Maybe later then,' he said to himself as he made his body disappear from where it was only to reappear on the beach in Heavenly Clacton.

He watched as the young woman splashed about in the sea before him. She eventually found her footing, so to speak, and swam towards the shore.

"Hello," said Chris as he held out his hand in a welcoming gesture and handed her the warm towel that he had been holding in his other hand. The woman looked up and after composing herself, said, "I know you, I have seen you before."

Chris smiled at her. "I am sure that you do, my child, we are after all, all linked to each other one way or another."

"I have seen pictures of you though, I know who you are."

"I hope that I don't displease you then."

"Is this it then; is this Heaven?"

"It all depends on what you believe."

"I was on the side of a river bank and then I was swimming in the sea, am I dead now?"

"I don't know, are you dead now, how do you feel?" asked Chris.

"I feel more alive than I have ever been," came the reply.

"There is your answer then."

"Is this Heaven?" asked the young woman.

"It is one version."

"Are there others here then?"

"Surely."

"Are there bad people in this heaven or have they gone to Hell?" asked the young woman.

"There is no hell, only differing versions of heaven," came the reply.

"What of the Devil, then, surely he is in charge of Hell and he looks after the bad people."

"We are all made from the same clay, some have strayed from the path but they go on, too, to their own heavens. Old Nick generally looks after them and steers them to where they should go, to make things right for themselves."

"What of Hitler then, is he here in this heaven that I have arrived in?"

"Do you want him to be?"

"No, I was only asking."

"You ask a lot, but in reply, no, Hitler does not live in this part of heaven."

"Then he is in hell, is he?"

"As I have said, there is no hell, only differing versions of heaven."

"He should rot in hell, he was the instigator and the killer of many."

"If you must know, he lives with the Jewish community, further along the coast, they are educating him about his wrongdoings and he is responding to their lessons of the past."

"I would have thought that he would have roasted in hell."

"Do you think that I should do that sort of thing, am I not all love? You need to rest a little before you are brought into the community."

"I have been wronged, I had to take a stand, and I had to do what I had to do."

"Walk with me," said Chris in a soothing manner and as they walked, Chris steered their journey towards the little café that sat on the beach. They entered and then took up a seat near a window where the sea could be seen.

Chris introduced the hurt young woman to the café's proprietor and left them to chat as they looked at the calming sea.

As Chris left the café, he looked through the window and saw that the young woman had streaming tears running down her face as she poured her heart out to Daphne, the proprietor of the café. 'Sometimes,' he thought to himself, 'we all need a woman's touch.'

Chris ambled along the beach and back through time a little, back to 1900 hours, as he reached home with the full intention of logging on and talking to Krishna.

As he arrived, Chris smiled once again at the wonders that kept jumping out in front of him.

'It is indeed a strange existence,' he thought to himself. Chris sat down before his computer and clasped his hands together. He then cracked his knuckles.

"Ouch!" said he, "I must stop doing that."

As he was about to log on to the computer, a calling came to him, 'Oh Dear, so far away too.'

Chris closed his eyes, focused his Soul and when he reopened his eyes he was sitting in a hospital ward, staring at the dying Antonio.

"Hello, Antonio," said Chris, as he appeared to only Antonio.

"Is that you Lord?" asked the sleeping Antonio.

"Yes, it is me, I have come to guide you on."

"Why me, Lord? I don't mean why me as in why is it my time to die, I mean why is it me that you choose to visit as I lie on my deathbed?"

"I try to meet all of the dying as they expire their last breaths in this world and then to guide them to the next to welcome them home."

"I will miss Stephie though, and I am sure that she will miss me, why do we have to part?"

"All things must pass, my friend."

"But it is so cruel, I love that woman."

"And she loves you in return."

"Why can't I stay with her then?"

"In a way, you can, you can watch from the other world as she continues in this one."

"I... I don't know, I am confused, why can't she come with me?"

"Would you like her to leave her life early, my son?"

"Well no, but..."

"All will become clear as we venture into the next world and rest assured that Stephanie will not forget you."

"Can I see her one last time before we go?" asked Antonio.

"Of course," and with these words, Chris allowed Antonio to appear, invisibly, within the hospital room. Stephanie stood looking through the room's window over towards the church; she had done all the weeping that she needed to do and now had calmed down slightly.

Antonio looked at her and smiled and then he looked at the corpse that he had left behind, that too seemed to have a faint smile on its lips.

He then looked towards the rear wall and at the picture of Lord Krishna on it.

"There is love in this room if you have a will to feel it," said Chris to Antonio.

"I can feel it and I know that Stephanie feels it too," came Antonio's reply.

"I bring love to the world where I can, I am love."

'I know you are, Lord, I can feel it, but why do you look like Krishna, silly me." That is how Antonio left this world, laughing at his own dream.

Chris smiled at what had just been said. 'Yes, we are alike, both in looks and in worth, we both bring love, as much love as we can and we send it on to the next life and we carry it with us and make sure that everyone, every spirit that we touch has its fair share of love, for without love, what is there to meld all the spirits in this endless void together.'

A short while later, Chris was once again walking on the beach in his Heavenly Clacton-on-Sea. He had dropped Antonio off at the Swan Inn, and was now heading home to his cottage to try once more to get in touch with Krishna.

As he walked along the beach, Chris looked out towards the sea and thought about how the light show should be for the beach party.

A floating stage perhaps, a few hundred yards out in the sea. Perhaps Thor could throw a few thunderbolts (thunderbolts are always better than mere fireworks). Perhaps Neptune could throw up some waves to go in tune with the thunderbolts. Perhaps Wagner could be persuaded to perform "Ride of the Valkyries" as an opener, it was always one of my favourites. Chris smiled to himself as he made the plans for the performance of an eternity time.

'For food though, who can we get to prepare the food?' thought Chris.

'Keith Floyd, that's the man, he does both meat and veggie dishes and he was very worldly-wise in his concoctions during his physical life, I must ask Krishna if he has any ideas on the food and any spirits he could recommend, it is going to be a wonderful party. Oh Krishna! You are so going to enjoy this party.'

AFSAL

ೞ

Unmindful of Christ's grand plans, Krishna went about his daily chores, living from one day to another. "Such is the grind of life," he was given to saying to the other pantry boys, his mates in the hospital. "Even the bare necessities come to us after a struggle; the incessant and unending struggle for existence." He had been waking up at three every morning to queue up for water at the municipality tap by the old banyan tree. He took turns with his mother to wait in the queue, going without sleep on some days. Water was scarce in summer; therefore the slums were supplied water at an hour when the rich had no use for it. In this very city men and women splashed water into the swimming pools to enjoy their summer sports while the poor killed each other for a mere bucket of water.

"Krishna, what's taking you so long to serve tea? As it is the days are insufferable, don't let the heat go to their heads. They are not ordinary guards, these are Black Cats! Do you know the importance of being a Black Cat commando? Black Cats are the most ferocious of all trained commandos which is why they guard the lives of these wicked politicians. Hurry up, my boy."

Sunderaman picked a cookie from the plate.

"If you take even one more cookie, I will serve tea without biscuits. I can't offer an empty plate to the minister's security personnel!" Krishna rearranged the biscuits again to make the plate appear full.

"Krishna, I tell you, you are taking wings. Don't forget it was I who got you here. Never bite the hand that feeds you, son." Sunderaman resisted picking up another biscuit.

"You have an entire store full of grub, why get me into trouble with these hunks? As it is they are a burly lot. They hauled up the guard at the gate who dared stop them to check their entry passes! Bloody rascals! I tell you, these goons in uniform."

"Oh we are 'beings of the gutter', my boy! What do you expect? If a terrorist were to kill us, right here, these trained Black Cats wouldn't budge from their post, because they are here to secure the lives of the politicians. And mind you, it is you and I who pay income tax to train them! Anyway, you and I will never amount to much in this world. These ministers have all the money, power, and women. Did you not see the sting video of that 73-year-old minister with three women, on TV! I have not had three women in my whole life and this bastard has three of them at one go." Sunderaman was not sure what he was angry about; the easy access ministers had to desirable women, or the sexless lives of the poor. There were homes where brothers, from dearth of money, were squeezed into one room with their families. These men had no more than a bedsheet for privacy when they had sex with their wives. Very often children could see their fathers humping their mothers because the poor could not afford separate rooms for their children. And not to mention here the poorest of the poor who sleep on pavements.

'This is inequality. It is the height of injustice,' Sunderaman thought to himself.

"Ha, ha! That old fellow needs three girls because he is not capable of much himself. You are a virile, young man, sir! The mere thought of a woman is enough for you! Now if you could get Sister Shiny that would be a real treat. Just be wary of that supervisor, Joana, she is beginning to sense your involvement."

Sunderaman put his arm around Krishna's shoulder in appreciation of the remark about his virility and then said, "Oh she's just a frustrated spinster, don't bother about her. We will tackle her later, Krishna. Meanwhile, you keep a close watch on Shiny. My boy, get me that girl and I promise, I will get you a permanent job in the department."

"What's up with you all? We have been waiting the whole day for a cup of tea!" a young commando from the minister's Special Protection Cover barged into the pantry. In his formidable presence Sunderaman felt threatened in his own domain. Inadvertently he shrank back, moving a step closer to the young and lusty pantry boy. Krishna, he noticed, remained unfazed and calm in all situations.

"And what is this then, sir?" Krishna balanced the tray laden with tea and cookies on his left palm and swerved the tray next to the bodyguard's face.

"Mind your step, boy! Next time I see you dancing around the place I will give you an enema with this tea! You don't know me, my juniors pee in their pants when I call out their names."

"There will be no next time for you or for me," Krishna walked past the conscript, his gait erect and confident and his mouth set in a firm expression. Sunderaman promptly offered butter cookies to placate the angry bodyguard. Later during the day, he accounted for that packet of biscuits in patients' rations.

"You fat man, tell that boy of yours not to mess with me! He must be darned lucky because the minister has decided to leave rightaway. If I had stayed a few more hours, I would have taught this cheeky boy a few lessons in humility," Afsal barked at Sunderaman, who was relieved to hear the minister's sudden change of plan.

"Are you all leaving, sir? What a pity! I was told that you will be here a couple of days. You know how it is with food. Like you we have to plan in advance, so we have all the latest updates. I am Sunderaman, manager in the food department. I had hoped to make a better acquaintance of you, sir. Never mind, we'll serve you better next time. You all look so brave, officer. I salute you and all Indian soldiers."

The sight of a fat man suddenly breaking into a salute amused Afsal. He smiled wryly and then gleefully, in one sweep, finished the remaining cookies in the packet.

The following day all national dailies carried headlines of a terrorist attack on a state minister of Jammu & Kashmir and his entourage. The news item elaborated that the deceased minister was in Delhi for secret parleys with the Central government. Heart ailment, it was said, was a red-herring to trick the media. Further, the news item speculated that the minister had ended the talks prematurely to express his disenchantment with the deal given to his regional party. All the Black Cat commandos on duty had died in the ambush trying to save the minister and his family.

Afsal was in far too much pain to reflect on his life that was about to end its course. He had wanted to pray but the young commando, who lay dying beside him, wallowed and wailed noisily. The young soldier saw his life slip away, slithering like an eel on a slippery surface. The other two commandos had passed out at the beginning of the ambush – it had always been like this in the past, some died in an instant.

Afsal felt a strange stillness in his heart; he was not sure what to think. 'What was there at the end of it,' he thought without remorse or curiosity. It did not matter, just then, that he had abused men and women, sexually and otherwise. It was incidental to him that he had killed many young men, even boys, to carry out the orders of the state. He felt no revulsion for his cruelty or abhorrence for his acts of violence committed during his lifetime. For some reason, in this moment of redemption, his mind flashed the face of the pantry boy at the hospital. He felt the gaze of the smiling boy skim his face. 'There will be no next time! How did he know?' he thought to himself. 'An unworthy pantry boy had no business showing up in his last hour, which was meant to be spent in contemplation and meditation,' he reminded himself.

He started to recite a prayer from the Holy Quran to do his last penance. He had only just begun when the mocking eyes of the pantry boy smiled in his mind.

"Bastard! Mother f******! How dare you mock me?" With an abuse on his lips, an angry Afsal passed into the next world.

The commanding officer, who arrived on the spot within hours of the incident, remarked to his subaltern, "Look at that expression, *uuf*! This is what I call an angry, patriotic soldier. Listen *jawan*, never forget this expression, never! I swear on your body, Afsal, we will not let this anger in our bellies die!"

Krishna did not want to use his Godly powers to connect with Christ; he enjoyed the drama of the Internet; this human business of leaving messages, replying to threads of commentary, and waiting to chat had a certain romance to it. The message read:

I missed you yet again, mate. Too many so-called VIPs to serve – work, my friend. How have you been faring? I am over-worked and tired, I think. Also, because I suspect that our work as Gods is becoming increasingly complex, as also liable to interpretation. Our primary job of judging human beings, and meting out to them in the next-life the rewards and punishments, is no longer as simple as it was. The idea of redemption mooted by your followers is too simplistic to apply, because we cannot absolve human beings of their *karma*; we are Gods, not parents. Even though a man seeks forgiveness, he cannot be condoned for pleading, alone.

Also, the notion of right and wrong in the human mind is determined by the law of the state and the social sanctions of the day. How can I punish adultery when I had many wives? And so did others – it was quite acceptable and 'right' then, so how can it be wrong now? Should we not rather examine the intent behind every action?

No one is fighting the battle of *Kurukshetra* anymore. Are atrocities not committed in the name of patriotism? When is it, my friend that killing another human being is fair? Even *dharma* is subject to interpretation.

For instance, consider Afsal – was he a patriot for killing young men who were perceived as terrorists by one faction and *jehadi* by the other? These soldiers are just as misled as the terrorists, and today the state is the perpetrator of the most heinous of crimes. If young

Muslim boys kill in the name of God, young soldiers slaughter to rise to the call of their duty. They are convinced of their convictions, both the sons of God and the sons of the soil. Religion has divided men so deep in their minds that they cannot tolerate another man's faith!

If I would be just in forgiving, then I would most certainly overlook the sins of mankind. How can I pardon *Duryodhana* upon asking forgiveness? Let's not forget that we have to face a *Draupadi* for every *Duryodhana* we forgive. Did I not punish *Karna*, the most noble of men, for desecrating a woman's honour?

You are right Chris, we are an exhausted lot – all us Gods. We need to let our hair down and party. Can we start the evening with a *Carnatic* music recital? Maybe later a jazz musician could humour us – but suit yourself buddy. Don't forget Buddy Roy hates loud music; I am more accommodating than him, lol.

Even though we love wines, and I trust you to arrange the best, still there are a few of us who prefer non-alcoholic beverages. Maybe you should arrange some fine English tea for them with home-made, eggless cookies. I know our demands are unreasonable, but that is called accommodating all faiths and views. Some of us are more ethical and mindful in our consumption of food.

Till we meet in person let's keep Facebooking, my friend. And you may get started with the preparations for the party, brother – I hope there isn't a dress code! All love.

ALMA

ဆ

A lma awoke and as she stared out towards the open sea in wonder, she was thrilled as the waves caressed her legs. 'What is going on?' she asked herself. She sat up and noted straightaway that her stomach did not hurt at all. Alma then felt at her throat for the self-inflicted wound. 'Nothing, that's odd,' she thought. She then looked at the waves as they washed over her lower legs. 'Where am I?'

Before dying, Alma had been an assassin, a hitman (one gender-bender, for sure), and a good one at that. She had built up quite a reputation as a killer and had made many kills. She and her boyfriend Frank the Fink had risen high in the ranks of assassins.

Alma had been chosen by the bosses to be sent on a hit alone though and had made a fatal mistake. That was why she found herself here.

As she looked around, she noticed a man standing a few feet away from her. He looked friendly enough and was smiling.

"Who are you buddy?" asked Alma, "and where am I?"

"My name is Ati, and you are lying on a beach Alma," returned the man with a smile.

"Before I passed out, I was lying in a pool of blood, I had been shot in the stomach and I was dying."

"And now you are here.

"And where is here?"

"Why, this is the Heavenly Frinton-on-Sea."

"What happened to my gunshot wound?" asked Alma.

"That gunshot wound helped to kill you my dear," came Ati's reply.

53

"Are you saying that I am dead then?"

"Well done. Yes, you are quite dead."

"Then why am I here, wherever here is?"

"All Souls have to go somewhere."

"Is this Heaven then?"

"One version of it," smiled Ati.

"Well there I have you then, I don't believe in the afterlife, I am an atheist."

"And I am Ati, the God of Atheists."

"You can't have a God of Atheists," laughed Alma.

"Then who am I?" asked Ati.

"I don't believe it, I absolutely refuse to believe in life after death or in any kind of God."

"By the very notion that you say that you don't believe, proves that you do believe in something. And that is why you are here, your very lack of belief produces me, and I am here to welcome you."

"This is quite unbelievable," said Alma in disbelief.

"Aha!" replied Ati.

Alma looked at her stomach, at where the wound should be. It was not there. Her skin was perfect and unblemished.

"Tell me, Ati, do I still have a scar on my cheek just to the right of my ear."

"Oh yes, that scar is still there."

"Then why is the wound that killed me not here?" she asked as she pointed to her stomach.

"Would you like it to be?" asked the God of Atheists.

Alma thought for a second or two, "No, no, I would not."

Ati looked along the beach and then out to the sea, "It is beautiful here on the coast, is it not Alma?"

Alma looked out at the crashing waves and smiled. She had to agree with him, it really was quite beautiful here. She had a thought.

"Tell me Ati, is Legitimate Leggy here?"

"Was he also an atheist?" asked the God.

"I don't know," came the reply.

"Well he may be, why don't we go and find out."

"You should know that if he is here, I will kill him."

"How will you do so Alma?"

"With a knife if I can find one, or a gun, or with just my bare hands?"

"There are no weapons here, my dear, and anyway how do you think you are going to kill anyone here, we are all already dead."

'Aha,' Alma thought and said, "Oh I see, he is dead already?"

"That's right."

"Then how can I punish him?"

"The easiest way is to show him as much love as you possibly can."

"But I hate him."

"Hate, too, is not allowed here."

"But," and as Alma butted, she burst into tears. Ati watched for a while and then said, "Alma, we have a welcoming party tonight in the big hall, Legitimate Leggy is here and he is in charge of the bar. You may enjoy yourself if you come. You don't have to if you don't want to, of course. For now though, I will guide you to your little retirement home, follow me."

Alma watched as the God walked off and then decided that it was probably best to follow, and so she went with Ati until he showed her the little cottage that was now hers.

"We will expect you at 1900 hours, there are plenty of clothes to change into, and I will see you later." Ati then faded into nothing and left Alma to get on with her new surroundings.

She walked into the little cottage and noted how well it had been decorated, it was quite to her taste and she approved of the décor. As she looked around the little cottage and admired all the rooms, she eventually came to the bathroom. 'This is nice,' she thought and then decided to draw herself a hot bath. She watched as the water flowed into the bath and as it flowed she added some bath salts that she had spotted on the shelf. She smiled as the bubbles started to rise. After testing the water, she settled into the bath and as she soaked, she considered all that had happened to her.

She was shot in the stomach. The bullet killed her instantly. Later, she had arrived on the beach of Frinton-on-Sea where she had been told by Ati, the God of Atheists, that she was dead. Then she had been presented with a new cottage and had been invited to a welcoming party, only to be told the man that she had killed would be there behind the bar. The same man who had killed her in their last fight. It had been a deadly encounter and both had been shot and had died.

After soaking herself for some time (she had realized that the bath's temperature remained constant), she towelled herself dry and then dressed for the party.

She chose a beautiful red dress. 'It will conceal the blood,' she thought to herself, and then applied her make-up. She then made her way to the big hall.

As she opened the door, she saw that the hall was crowded and behind the bar, Legitimate Leggy seemed happy as he served drink after drink to the revelers. Alma walked over to the bar and stared Leggy in the face, "Gin and Tonic, Leggy." Legitimate Leggy looked at Alma.

"I wondered when you would get here," he said with a smile, "there seems to be some sort of time delay."

"Well I am here now, love," came her reply. "Why don't you come out from behind that bar and give me a welcoming cuddle?"

"All right," replied Leggy with a smile as he lifted the flap and walked from behind the bar towards Alma. As he approached Alma, she stretched her arms and as he got nearer, she put her hands around Leggy's throat and squeezed. Leggy moved forward slightly so her hands went through his throat in a ghostly manner and then he put his arms around her and cuddled her. Alma's own hands now returned to normal as she placed them on the back of Leggy's neck. She tried to squeeze again but her hands again faded.

In an instant, Ati was by her side, "As I told you Alma, you cannot kill what is already dead."

"Then what is the point of it all?"

"That is for you to decide."

"But if we can't kill, how do we avenge ourselves?"

"We don't."

"But how then do we strive? Who becomes the leader? We all need wealth after all."

"Everyone is equal here, Alma and everyone has what they need."

"I don't believe in this and I don't believe in you."

"That's why we are here, Alma, if you believed then you would not be here, you would be elsewhere."

"Who are you?"

"I have told you, I am Ati, the God of Atheists."

"This is all wrong," cried Alma, "it is not what I expected at all."

"It can change over time. In time you may be able to move on."

"Move on, move on to where?"

"This is only one part of Heaven; there are other parts as well. At the moment you do not believe and so you are here."

"But what of you, do you believe?"

"Why of course I believe."

"Then why are you here, how can you be the God of Atheists and believe too?"

Ati stared at Alma for a moment before he said, "When I first came here I too was an unbeliever, an Atheist, but as time went on I came to believe. I have met the creator and so I not only believe, but I know."

"Then why are you still here, why have you not moved on?"

"Ah, that is an easy one. My term of office is not yet over, I have two more weeks to go and then I am off to the heavenly version of Clacton-on-Sea, to be with the one that I believe in."

"But then there will be no God of Atheists, what happens then?"

"I have not explained too well, have I, the God of Atheists is nothing more than a title really, and an honorary position. It is held for as long as it takes for a person to convert his beliefs. I found out what I believe to be the truth long ago and so my term of office will soon be up."

"And then what?" asked the disbelieving Alma.

"Well believe it or not, Legitimate Leggy has said that he would like to hold the honorary title of Ati next."

"I don't believe it."

"There you go again, Alma. Over time, you will come to believe, but there is no rush."

"I don't think that I will ever believe."

"Some never do, but they are few and far between, you will believe one day, I am sure of it."

"What of Frank the Fink, will he turn up here some time?"

"Is he an Atheist too, Alma?"

"I don't know, I think that the only thing that Frank believes in is Frank."

"Then he may well turn up here sometime but time can be fickle, it moves in mysterious ways."

"Then I will wait for him."

"Well, it is a pleasant area to wait in, the waters are warm and the people are friendly, enjoy your stay Alma, I have to go now as I have my own party to go to," and with these words the current Ati faded.

"Another drink Alma?" asked Legitimate Leggy.

"Why not?" replied Alma, "Leggy, what's happening here, you are a killer, why have you accepted this?"

"When you have stayed here for a while you will see it all clearer, then you will understand."

"You could not have been here much longer than me, how come you understand?"

"I think that there is some kind of time lapse, and I grasped the concept really quickly. Oh and happiness helps."

"But you always wanted wealth to pay for your retirement."

"I have it now."

"What do you have, you are working behind a bar."

"I volunteered, I am happy to do this, you will understand one day."

"I don't think that I will ever understand but I will wait for Frank, then perhaps we will be able to sort this thing out together."

"Maybe you will Alma, but for now, just enjoy the night and the music, you may even meet a new fellow, who knows."

"Frank's my man, I will wait for him."

"Eternity can be a long time Alma, time can certainly fool you here."

"I will wait Leggy, I will wait for Frank."

The music played, the drinks flowed, and the party carried on into the early hours.

Time moved on a little.

Over in Clacton-on-Sea, Chris leaned back and stretched out his hands. As he did this, he clasped his hands together and was just about to crack his knuckles when he thought to himself, 'No, it is time of change.'

He had been logged onto the computer station and realized that yet again he had missed his old friend. Getting in touch over the Internet did indeed have its romance.

Chris read the last posting on his wall by Krishna and the thoughts of times past came to the fore. As someone once commented, "Sometimes, memories are better than dreams." Chris sat for a moment and let his thoughts traverse his mind. His hands then found the keyboard and he then typed his next communiqué to Krishna.

Hello, old friend, of course all types of beverages will be served. I, myself, am quite partial to a strange brew called "Earl Grey Tea", and I will happily sip and talk to you as we watch this fascinating get-together unfold. Some jazz, you ask, well I am sure that the old reprobate "George Chisum" could be enticed to perform a tune or two, he was always one of my favourites. As for the *Carnatic*, I think that I would be happier if just the two of us shared this music before the festival itself starts, we could just sit and listen together as we did when we were young. Buddy Roy could sit in with us too. Bacchus is now in charge of the bar, I thought that this was a good idea, as he will probably drink most of the alcohol before the party starts. We have many chefs from all over the world, and from all times, to prepare all kinds of food. A taste to suit everyone. It will be nice to sit down and talk to all our other contemporaries about how the heavens and men are changing. After all, we are all Gods.

As for the dress code, Krishna, you were always so formal. Come as you please. I, myself, will just be in jeans and wearing my Panama hat, as it will be a hot day.

The date for the party we can set in the English summer. I hope to see you then but before then, let's just try to talk via the Internet. I will log in again later and hope that you too are logged in at the same time so that we can connect.

I love you, my friend.

SHINY

৪৩

Sunderaman had taken to compulsive snacking in order to distract his mind, which was caught in a vortex of fantasy. To him food was the next likeable thing after sex. In some ways his libido found its compensation in desserts. His *objet de desire* was out of bounds not so much for socio-moral conventions as for his ungainly, obese form. Wherever he went he evoked ridicule and repulsion for his enormous size. But, to his credit, Sunderaman was not an easy man to dissuade, nor could he be pushed away gently.

Shiny's mild rebuffs did little to dampen his obsessive stalking. She was a girl who knew her mind, but was far too polite and gentle in her ways to rebuke a fat man for following her around. Sunderaman had the grace to refer to lust as love, a euphemism that he was beginning to believe in himself.

Krishna strolled into his office on one such afternoon, when Sunderaman was aching with love.

"Here sir, write it down before you forget; two packets of Marie biscuits, one pack of tea bags, and one litre of unconsumed milk."

Krishna scrutinized Sunderaman's blanched face. So the gossip had reached him?

"Have you heard about the new doctor yet? The one who recently joined the same ward as hers? I have only second-hand information, and I don't trust the fellow who told me whatever he did. Besides, some gossip or the other is always doing the rounds in the wards; I don't know what to believe?" Krishna unloaded his trolley while talking to what looked like, a crest-fallen Sunderaman.

"They are such a waste, all these nursing aides. All they do is spread malicious rumours about someone or the other. After all, nurses and doctors are colleagues. They work as a team, don't they?"

Krishna felt sorry for Sunderaman despite the fact that he was cheating his wife in spirit. Krishna reflected at the convoluted destiny of men; they married one and loved another. The God felt for Sunderaman's pain though his love was more erotic than romantic. Sunderaman was in throes of passionate attraction. Affection and gentle feelings were not part of his nature. Yet he was tormented by his state of love. Krishna, the God, had a soft spot for all lovers – be it the boors or the poets, Gods love lovers.

Sunderaman reached for another packet of biscuits; involuntarily he tore the packet open and flicked the contents into his huge mouth. He abused the world at large, muttering expletives randomly and directing them at nobody in particular. And then for a minute he hated Shiny most of all. He despised her for inflicting pain and shame on him. He hated her like he had never hated anyone. He was willing to reconcile to her rejection of his love advances; but now to show preference for another was unbearable! He recalled how he had waited to catch a glimpse of her face, how he had spent hours thinking about what he would say to her. And now the memory of his own love tormented him.

Krishna smiled again at the thought that even the cruelest of men suffer in love. Sunderaman looked miserable, tearful, and shame-faced in this moment. Oh! How his heart ached now!

"Sir, how should we use these little darlings that have aged before time?" Bheem sauntered in with a specimen of an overripe pulpy mango that was beginning to rot at the top. On another day Sunderaman would have hurled abuses at his junior for waving a mango at him, but today he merely gave Bheem a look of disapproval.

"I don't think we can give this to the patients," Bheem continued with enthusiasm. He was much too excited at the prospect of drinking mango shake to be dampened by another man's gloom.

"Why, you look rather glum today!" he said with some feeling.

"I am in a foul mood, Bheem, don't mess with me. Don't you imagine you can eat these mangoes; we will use the whole lot in the pudding. Only last week all of you had mango shake, now no more. All you guys want is free grub – now get lost and put the mango on my table! Wait till I pull up the supplier; how is it that mangoes don't last even three days in cold storage!"

Sunderaman had used his discretion, the week before, to write off five kilos of putrefying mangoes. But today, he felt the world had no right to be happier than him.

"They don't look as bad as last week's lot!" Krishna sniffed the 'specimen mango' to humour his boss.

Mango shake was a rare treat for pantry boys who were entitled to one free meal at the hospital. Fruits, desserts and other delicacies were reserved for the patients' and doctors' mess. Last week the pantry boys had had a good run of luck because not only had the mangoes deteriorated significantly, but Sunderaman had then been upbeat about what he had imagined was a smile from Shiny.

Bheem, the helper to the Senior Chef, was undaunted by Sunderaman's outright rejection of his suggestion. "But should you not check with madam before using them? After all, we have to feed vulnerable patients of the privileged class. Even at the peak of their health they cannot digest overripe stuff. Their bodies are not like ours. Most of us can drink water from the gutter, straight; I reckon we are made of different stuff." Bheem picked up the mango and hurled it high in the air to exhibit its state of ripeness. Krishna caught the fruit before it squashed on Sunderaman's table. He examined it closely and as he put it down on the table he thought he saw a tear drop fall onto the table.

Later that evening when Krishna sat in front of the desktop in the doctors' room, he remembered Sunderaman's bloated, helpless face. The sight of a boor-turned-melancholic lover was pitiably comical.

His thoughts then returned to the Internet as he noticed that Chris had not yet logged on to Facebook for a chat. 'Another day, then,' thought Krishna as he typed a reply.

Hello, friend. I am sorry; I can't linger indefinitely to keep our appointment tonight. I have to accompany my mother to the Kali temple. It kind of cropped up today, out of nowhere. I suspect my mother had avowed to offer coconut to Goddess Kali the day my father died. Or maybe he has come to some harm, I don't know. Or let us say, I choose not to know. She is, like any other human being, entitled to privacy and her inner life. I don't even view this as meanness in her character; a victim is morally justified in cursing his or her tormentor. That man used and discarded her for mere pleasure, why should she pardon him? Destiny is the greatest equalizer, my friend, who knows it better than us? And who can a woman count on, if not Kali?

Love is a strange thing, it makes you humble. I have always surrendered to love; there was never another Radha for me, not even my wife. It is man's innate nature to love and create. It's no small wonder that he is so dear to me. Has he not created great art and verse? And drama, the greatest of arts, is my personal favourite. I still marvel at the mind that wrote *Oedipus Rex* or the poet who penned *Abhigyana Shaakuntalam* – man, my own creation, has bettered me. I cannot, for the life of me, write like Sophocles, Shakespeare, or even Harold Pinter! Really, man has done us proud!

But then it's also his innate nature to destroy; did we not plant that seed of discontent in him? Eros and Thanatos; man's dual nature; life and death; they are the same thing, my friend. Greed and unrest in today's world is manifestation of his destructive instinct. Environment is protesting against man's greed! Don't you agree that natural calamities are his own making? And yet, when it all comes to an end, I will miss the most wonderful of my creations! We both know, you and me that everything that is born must die. But before that End we have to meet! So long, my friend.

Xx

The world turned a little and Christ and Krishna continued their daily strife as they carried on with the day job of trying to keep the world afloat and of course the Heavens afloat also. It was indeed an enormous balancing act.

Sometime later, as Chris checked his mail he thought, 'Krishna is disappointed indeed. What about the other Hindu Gods, though. Shiva has been restless too. Is it the beginning of another tragedy?" Chris was now beginning to worry.

Shiva's Walk of Death.

He had not been happy of late and as such he had taken himself off for a walk. . Chris saw him in his mind's eye. Chris watched Shiva walk into the ocean and as he walked he stamped his feet on the face of the Earth. He did not really mean any harm by this, after all Shiva is a confused God. Why else would he tie up his hair into a knot on the top of his head, for centuries? Even Gods need to maintain personal hygiene.

Shiva walked through the bottom ground of the ocean and as he walked he stamped and this stamping caused the plates beneath the Earth to collide, and as they collided and scraped, a huge tsunami was created. This tsunami was aimed at an island in the Far East. Shiva was oblivious to this happening, he just looked ahead of himself as he walked on, lost in thought. He was watched though. Oh yes, he was watched. Chris sent him telepathic messages to stop the 'walk of death', but Shiva was shut out to telepathy and reason. Chris watched and worried.

Old Nick, The Devil, himself sat on high, looking down at Shiva as he walked. As he saw that the stamping had created a tsunami, Nick wove his old magic and pointed the great wave at the Far Eastern island that contained a nuclear reactor. 'This should be fun,' thought he.

The wave hit the island and washed away houses and cars, cattle and people all over the place. Waves so high, that cars were swept up onto the very rooftops of houses; waves so high that people were swamped and died in an instant. Waves eager to devour all that stood in its path.

The wave washed over the island and hit the nuclear reactor. Shiva felt this foundation shaking and not to be outdone, he stamped his foot again, causing the beginning of yet another tsunami.

Many people died this day and as they died, Old Nick smiled at what he had accomplished.

"Why do you smile so?" asked Chris as he floated in the morning sky beside Old Nick.

"Oh, so it's you, you really made me jump a little with your instant appearance, why are you here?"

"To be fair Nick, I was happily reading an email on my computer when I realized what was happening. And I thought straightaway that I should come to see if I could save any lives or at least salvage something from this monstrosity that has been released."

"Too late for that, Chris, far too late. The chaos that has been released has done its job."

"Why do you do these things, Nick?" asked Chris.

"It wasn't me, chap, it was Shiva, he is the one who stamped his feet and caused this to happen."

"You directed its path though, Nick, why did you do this thing?"

"Why do you care, all humans suffer and must suffer, I have just given a few of them an early release from their suffering and anyhow, this deed will fill up our respective coffers, some souls for you and some for me."

"It's not the way of things, Nick, it's not how it should happen. Just to snuff out life is not right, our Father said that the humans should be allowed to continue and to make their own decisions and find their own paths."

"You too snuff out life, I have seen you do it."

"Only when it is necessary, and I welcome the souls as they come over to the heaven that they want."

"Your vision of heaven is not the same as mine, the humans need to be sorted out, numbered and catalogued as their souls come over, for too long now you have just let them do as they please."

"Nick, is this not what heaven should be about?"

"No, it is too chaotic, we need order."

"Father said that all things should be allowed to grow in their own ways."

"Father was wrong."

"Nick, I am going to stop this wave now for the sake of the children."

"You always do have to interfere and spoil my fun," replied Old Nick as he disappeared from view.

Chris looked at the spot where Old Nick had been sitting and thought to himself, 'I do wish that you would just grow up and take some sort of responsibility for the souls that you take.'

Chris then looked out towards the sea and wondered how Krishna was getting on with Shiva. He just had to contact him through the old channels, the Internet would be no use for something as big as this but, of course, Krishna would have known instantly that the tsunami had begun, of what was happening.

"I wonder how the two of them are getting on," he thought to himself.

GODS TOGETHER

&

In another part of the universe, two other Gods were conversing, The Buddha floated as he looked in peace at the sea below him.

"Hello, Buddy Roy," said Old Nick in a loud voice as he appeared in front of the Buddha.

The Buddha slowly opened his eyes and smiled as he looked at the being before him.

"I made you jump for sure just then, did I not Roy?"

The Buddha just smiled and continued with his concentration.

"Well, say something Roy, are you as deaf to the nothingness that is this everlasting life as the rest of the Gods?"

The Buddha looked before him and smiled as he said, "You are so young Nick and have so much to learn, why don't you just slow down a little and try to enjoy your existence."

"I am not so young, I am nearly 3,000 years old now."

"A mere blink of the eye of the great one, you are so young."

"You are younger than me."

"I may be younger in the real terms of age, but I have learned to take things in my stride, I enjoy every waking moment of existence."

"You worry too little and do nothing to make things happen."

"You are wrong, my young friend, I just appear to do nothing, but underneath this veil of serenity, I work very hard to keep the life force of existence balanced."

"Why do we bother, why do you bother? Why should I not just do away with as many humans as I can?"

"What will you do without humans, Nick?"

"Wait, this needs explaining. I will create a better species than humans and make Earth as abundant as Heavens. All my subjects would live their lives to the full, no death, no hardships like hunger or thirst, all would be equally looked after if they just worshipped me."

"How long do you think you could live like this, Nick, how long before you are bored by all this worship, is it not better just to support the living in their struggles and keep the life force going?"

"I am bored with it all now; I would destroy it all if I could," said The Devil.

"You are a young God, Nick, come, sit by my side and meditate with me."

"I don't have time to waste in sitting about with you, I will go back down to the Earth and give these mortals the miracles that they seek."

"What miracles, Old Nick? Will you show them conjuring tricks, will you become a mage or magician? Will you try to blind them with tricks as you seek their love?"

"I am bored as I said, I will do as I please. Rock the Universe, make tsunamis, flood rivers, burst volcanoes – we will we will rock you," Nick sang, banging his head and dancing to the song.

"Sit with me, Nick, you will experience peace at my side."

"Come with me, Roy, you will be exhilarated as I create chaos wherever I go."

"You are so different from your brother Chris."

"He is like you, he has no passion."

"The Christ as The Krishna is the most passionate being that I have ever known. You should perhaps try to be more like them. But in your own way I suppose that you are; as you too have passion."

"Roy, I thought that you may understand me better than the others but it appears that I am wrong. I am off," and with that Old Nick disappeared.

Buddha took a deep breath and continued on his way through existence. As he carried on his way, he concentrated as much of his energy as he could as he focused peace and love towards the Earth.

DR. AMARJEET

❧

Dr. Amarjeet had been in the dialysis room all night and a good part of the morning too. His muscles ached from being on constant vigil, and his eyes strained hard to stay awake. 'If I could get away from the room somehow,' he said to himself over and over again. He hadn't so much as gone out of the ICU for a minute in the last 12 hours. 'Damn! Why can't we go out for a leak!' he cursed the hospital authorities while zipping up his fly in the toilet. Toilets had been provided within the Unit so as to confine the 'on-duty' doctors and nurses to the sterile zone of the Dialysis Unit. Only when someone manipulated the door, to come in or leave, did a whiff of fresh air sneak in. Dialysis machines needed strict temperature control and a dust-free environment, making it mandatory to curtail human traffic in the area.

Dr. Amarjeet was a young, sociable Sikh with an MBBS degree and an immense liking for Indian curries and deep-fried snacks.

'Dialysis Unit' duty was especially difficult for a man like him, who was used to snacking every few hours. He sighed, yet again, at the thought of having to spend another hour in confinement.

Krishna brought with him the smell of beverages and food into the room that reeked with the smells of medicine and blood. Patients scarcely took notice of the comings and goings. They were too dazed with pain, caused by needles and tubes that pierced their arms, to notice life about them.

"*Eh*, Krishna! Do you have some tea on you, my boy?" Dr. Amarjeet asked, without giving much thought to the implication of his question. He did not realize that what looked like harmless pinching of food, was no school-boyish prank; it was a serious offence liable to legal action against him and Krishna. Krishna quickly made a reply to salvage the situation, "Don't pull my leg, sir. I am a small man; I will lose my job because of your jokes. Here, Mini *Chechi*, don't you now go around telling people that Krishna passes on patients' food to doctors," Krishna grinned at Sister Mini, who was as disinterested in the conversation that had been going on between him and Amarjeet, as the birds are in human talk. All she cared for was to escape to Dubai so as to be able to earn the dowry for her marriage.

Mini's parents had spent their savings on her college education, which enabled her to qualify as a nurse. Now that she had a job with a hospital, they expected her to clear her debt by providing for her siblings, who were much too young to earn for themselves. Unlike other Indian parents of girls her age, her family was not anxious about finding her a groom. Hence marriage was her own private mission to accomplish – right from finding a boy to arranging the dowry.

"Why *Chechi*, you are forever caught in a vortex of thoughts! Good, you didn't hear our little chit-chat." Krishna beamed a smile at the nurse.

"Don't trouble me Krishna; you don't want me to report you to the sister supervisor! I have no time to waste on any chit-chat," she snapped at him, without stopping the flow of her movement. There were far too many chores to finish, making it impossible for the nurses, posted in an ICU, to exchange polite pleasantries with the other staff. Amarjeet, on the other hand, was tired after an exacting night-shift, and Krishna's inane jokes provided necessary relief from the morbid world of haemodialysis and patients.

"What news of the world Krishna? Sister Mini and I have been confined for over ten hours now. I hope the world outside this door is the same as yesterday," Amarjeet enquired not from curiosity, but out of a need to talk to someone who was not as over-worked and laconic as the nurse-on-duty.

"This world is a strange place; within a fraction of a second we may move in infinite worlds, from the outer to the inner to the outer. You know how it is; but now, where do we start from, maybe we should start with the immediate world outside this room. The ward, the nursing station, the ward nurses, my pantry are all the same as last evening. Now let's move further; as we step out of the hospital this world gives way to other worlds. Do you remember the beggar at the bus stop, outside the hospital? He died last night, from God knows what! You couldn't have missed him; he used to be bang outside the hospital gate at five. A funny fellow he was, conceding concessions to the hospital employees. 'I accept one rupee alms only from you guys, the going rate these days is two rupees. I know you are all underpaid,' he would say to us. He enjoyed chatting with us even though we had no money to give away." Krishna continued his speech after a sigh, "And further down, at the Khanpur-crossing, there was yet another accident." He spoke slowly, in a calm, bass voice, withholding bits of information, and divulging reluctantly. His words and the tenor of his voice caught the attention of the harried nurse and the resigned patients.

"Oh that crossing is jinxed!" said Sister Mini. "Every Sunday we cross that road, with trepidation and fear, to attend the Sunday mass." She lifted the cross to her lips and muttered a prayer.

"Was it bad?" Amarjeet asked dispassionately.

"Bad? Yes. Very bad. No survivors. It is the second 'container' accident in a month," Krishna spoke like a magician who had more secrets up his sleeve.

The nurse gasped in horror and the rosary around her neck found its way to her lips.

"Imagine a 12-metre-long container truck, weighing 3,000 kilos on its own, with God knows how many kilos of loaded freight, slipping off the truck trailer and landing on a mini bus! Can you imagine what became of the bus, or even human beings inside the bus? And what's more, even though every single one of the passengers died on the spot, yet they had to be taken to the Government Hospital, 20 kilometres away, to be declared dead! Such is the life of the poor, sir; our life is not worth a penny!" Krishna's audience was still and reflective.

"It has nothing to do with wealth, Krishna. My life comes as cheap as yours; it's about being a common man. A common man's life does not amount to much in this country, so let's enjoy ourselves till we are clinically alive." Amarjeet marvelled at his own words. He was not one to delve into the depths of anything serious; his life was one pursuit of hedonistic pleasures. Though, of late, for some inexplicable reason he found himself reflecting on life's existential questions.

"Oh yes, let us humour ourselves with *samosas*, cricket, and drink fizz to the ICC Cricket World Cup," Krishna spoke with a wry smile and started to clear the tables by the side of patients' beds to place the drinks he had brought from the pantry for the patients. Just as he was about to leave, he turned abruptly to face Amarjeet, "By the way, did you hear of the earthquake and tsunami that hit Japan? Many dead and many more missing – everyone is glued to their television sets; even the very sick are feeling fortunate today." Krishna had left before Amarjeet could comprehend the import of his words.

"Oh, my God, an earthquake! And did he say tsunami! Shit! That's major news, and all this while he withheld it from us. That's the thing; you don't get to know a thing in here! Why can't we have television sets here or at least a radio?" Amarjeet felt excitement and fear creep into his being.

"Lord, have mercy! They must be showing it live on TV, no?"

At last, Mini put away her work. She stared out of the window and all her worries about her marriage, dowry, and finding love vanished. 'Why do you want so much from life when most are given so little?' she heard a voice in her mind, loud and clear.

"Did Krishna return?" she asked Dr. Amarjeet.

"No, why do you ask?" Amarjeet felt he could do with some talk on this day.

"Don't know why, but I thought I heard his voice. Maybe I was hallucinating!" Mini returned to the nursing station to resume work.

"You know what, radio is our basic human right. These working conditions are driving us insane. We cannot be expected to remain unconnected to the world for 12 hours at a stretch. Even the telephone signals are weak here. Did you know Sister that in some countries social media is now acknowledged as a basic human right? Come to think of it, I haven't been on Facebook for two days now! But wait, Sister, did we get the consent form signed by Anurag's attendant? No? Listen, I want that damn form now, quickly page her, call her, do something!"

Amarjeet and Mini got on with their jobs. They forgot about the tsunami, the accident that had crushed all the passengers under a cargo container, and also the beggar who had died suddenly without a reason. They only remembered the calls of their duty, their personal dreams, and their small ambitions.

MIRACLE FLIGHT

&

K rishna was angry. 'It is not Shiva alone,' he thought, 'all the Gods are in connivance over earth's end, but it is Shiva who takes the blame. All this because he is given to anger more than any other God; or maybe he is fed up of man's arrogance.'

Looking down from the terrace, Krishna watched the swarm of men and women jostling with a never-ending stream of cyclists to cross the road; each in a great hurry to reach his destination.

Krishna resumed his soliloquy, 'In such a hurry to go places, and then one day they have to leave it all. Unwilling to live a life of quiet existence, disinclined to live in prayer and meditation, always chasing a thrill. Oh Man! You are evolving backwards! How can you be happy in the gross sensual experience? It is a decaying civilization where women are desperate to fix anything that shows signs of sagging and men are besotted with their own phallus!

'Man, my most precious creation, you amuse me no end. Just like little children create a make-believe fairy world for their play, you have created microcosms of self-glory. And you call it by motley names – the world of theatre, the world of fashion, the world of commerce, and last of all, the world of commoners. And I created you equal! You spend your entire life creating distractions like music and art. Aren't you the living characters of Adamov's *Le Ping-Pong*? For one there's the Ping-Pong of cinema, for another the Ping-Pong of football! How many Ping-Pong games does a man need?'

On this day Krishna felt the chasm between him and the human race widen. He could no longer forgive man's flaws, even though he loathed his own insolence and cruelty.

The hospital terrace was his 'escape-zone'; he came here when he was tired of it all. The days he found himself in concurrence with other Gods he escaped to the terrace to reflect in solitude – 'Man has outlived his term. May his toys kill him, and his own contraptions become a death trap!'

When he stepped away from the world, and detached himself from the *avatar* of a pantry boy, it seemed only natural that the world should end. Shiva's *tandav* is preordained, he reasoned with himself.

Just then, Sunderaman's vocal chords exerted hard to scream an alert to, what appeared to him to be, a man on the brink of suicide. He had been waiting for a delivery van when Sunderaman spotted a man on the hospital roof, a good seven floors up from the ground.

"*Oye*! Step back! Move back, not even half a step forward – hey, somebody, help him!" No sooner had Sunderaman drawn attention to the man on the terrace than frenzy took over the hospital. Guards ran from their posts, somebody pressed an alarm bell, and another group of security personnel dashed to the terrace. There had been three suicides in the last two years. All the men who had jumped to death had been both poor and in the last stages of a painful disease. In the wake of these unfortunate incidents, the hospital authorities had issued a strict leash to the guards and the nursing staff to maintain strict vigilance, at all times, in order to avert any mishap in future.

"How did he reach the terrace, it's a breach. All the doors to the terrace are locked and all the windows in patients' rooms are sealed from outside; there is no way a man can get there without a set of keys!" the security-in-charge reported to the medical director. He asked for a stand-by medical team, and rushed a team of rescuers with a set of keys to the terrace. Meanwhile a crowd had gathered from nowhere around Sunderaman, who had first spotted the suicidal man.

"Either he is in the throes of a disease with no money to pay the bills, or he is a jilted lover," an onlooker remarked to Sunderaman, who stood like a hero in front of the crowd.

"Love is a sad thing, never love these women, I tell you. Treat them like whores, never feel an iota of emotion for them – look what they have done to that poor man, whoever he is. Hey brother! Stay there, forget the damn whore, life will move on, and women will roll on the floor to have you. Look at his graceful, muscular body!" Sunderaman pointed out the man to the public at large, and for the first time they looked at the man in admiration.

Sunderaman regaled the onlookers with his antics and melodrama, calling out to the man on the terrace one moment and addressing the crowd the other minute. He was pleased to have drawn attention to himself. The crowd, on the other hand, was thrilled with the unfolding of the action. Most of these men who had gathered had too much time and too little occupation to engage their minds with. And it is for this reason that cricket and reality-shows were a hit with them. And here was real action – the struggle between a man intent on killing himself and a team of rescuers who would not let him die.

"*Hey Ram*! He has jumped!" somebody screamed from among them, and within a second the crowd dispersed. Before they knew it, however, the man on the terrace had reversed his course of trajectory; he had flown up into the skies instead of crashing down. The only person who saw the spectacle clear and vivid was none other than the self-appointed commentator. In that brief moment, a mist separated the man from the crowd – later the onlookers could only recall a strange, blue mist. By some divine play Sunderaman was the only one allowed to see through the mist.

Sunderaman saw the man on the terrace spread out his arms like wings, look up to the dull grey skies above, and for a second Sunderaman imagined that the man smiled down at him, and then took off like a space missile, straight up! Most onlookers imagined they had seen something like a bird or an animal fly. And still some other witnesses were not sure. Later, the crowd cursed Sunderaman for having fainted and fallen on another bystander, half his size, just when the man on the terrace had vanished into the skies. For a minute, everyone in the crowd thought that it was the man on the terrace who had fainted, and in this confusion they had missed what had later come to be referred to as, a 'miracle flight'.

Hospital authorities insisted that it was only a huge animal or a bird that had flown in from a neighbouring bird-sanctuary. Only that the bird-sanctuary was nothing more than an un-inhabited area with some newly planted trees, awaiting the arrival of birds. But the hospital administration had the lock on the door of the terrace to prove that the security had not been breached, and also that all the patients along with their attendants were accounted for and alive.

No one, except Sunderaman, had actually seen the 'miracle flight'. Sunderaman was prescribed a week's rest for nervous exhaustion. Later, on his return, he found that Krishna had left the city. No one was unduly worried or suspicious because Krishna had a track record of disappearing at least once a year. He left without a reason and returned without an apology; no one knew where he went or why he returned. Upon returning he would scurry their queries, parry all pokes, laugh away insinuations, and amuse them with the tales of distant lands, which they would never see for themselves.

FARAWAY ISLAND IN EAST

৪৩

Krishna vanished from one world to be in another. He roamed the deserted roads of a far away island in the East. The distant island had been hit by the tsunami, which had then caused a nuclear reactor to leak radiation. Krishna had taken on the avatar of a monk, to slip into his new surroundings. He helped with his bare hands, healed with some magical herbs tucked away in his robes, and buried the dead with a prayer. When he vanished after a few months, people referred to him as the handsome monk. Little did they realize that no one had enquired about his whereabouts, and also that he had never broached the subject of who he was or where he came from.

For a few months that followed, Krishna lost touch with the rest of the Gods. When he came face to face with man's suffering he forgot that his friends had an agenda to finish mankind. He sent a message to Christ via telepathy – "I wish I could remain unfazed like the other Gods and leave man to his destiny. I am here, in the Far East, in an astral body. I keep many bodies because I am needed everywhere at the same time. I suppose being a God has its advantages. What are you thinking, my friend? Of course, I will be there for the party, don't you worry on that account. And I promise I will come in my physical body, that is, as physical as our bodies can be.

P.S.- My friend, today I am ashamed to be a God! Godliness, as it stands today, has streaks of coldness and cruelty! This is not my idea of Gods' nature."

CHAN AND JO LEE

૮౩

A telepathic reply was returned.

"I was there too, my friend. I too healed as I walked through this unhappy place. Healed who I could, and helped others on their way to the next life. I tried to prevent even more mortal death from the on-going disaster scene. I watched you when I could, as you carried out your own healing. I could see the burden that you carried; I could feel that burden too, as I carried some of it for you. Did you not notice the monk who followed your path and tried to do as much good as you did? Perhaps you were too engrossed in the good work that you were doing to realize that others were there as well. Others, too cared for the sick, injured, dying and dead. You are not alone in your suffering, my friend. I too hurt as I walk through my existence."

As the Gods walked along the places where the disaster had struck, mere mortals were carrying on with what had befallen them. Jo Lee was at this very moment looking for her one true love. Some weeks before this incident, her lover, Chan, had spoken of how much he loved her and of how he wanted them to spend the rest of their lives together. It seemed now that his wish had come true.

Two weeks earlier, Jo Lee and Chan had sat on the mountain that overlooked the sea. These two lovers were so tied up in each other's presence, so much in love were they that they did not even notice the world as it turned.

Jo Lee smiled as she looked into Chan's eyes, he moved his mouth forward towards hers.

"Not here Chan," said Jo Lee, coyly, "people are watching."

"What people, we are alone here on this mountain."

"The people that are my ancestors are watching over me."

"Well, let them watch and if they disapprove, let them say something," laughed Chan as he planted a big smacker of a kiss on Jo Lee's lips. Jo Lee bit deep into Chan's bottom lip and drew blood.

"Ouch!" cried Chan, but he too bit into Jo Lee's lip and drew blood. For is it not said that if love comes along and bites you, you should bite straight back or be locked in its mouth forever and it is then that you will suffer.

These two lovers laughed as they bled together and then kissed together playfully.

"I love it when you bite me Jo."

"I love it when you bite me back," replied Chan. "We can go on forever you know, Jo."

"Do you think that we can, do you think that we will?"

These two young lovers kissed and carried on with their early exploration of each other and there on the mountain, as these two enjoyed themselves, the God known as Old Nick looked down from up above and smiled in a knowing, mischievous way. Time moved on and the worlds turned.

Jo Lee and Chan had many, many nights together, secret nights, known only to themselves as they enjoyed their young lives and explored each other in that innocent way that youth has. On the day of the great tsunami that struck their island, these two were embraced in each other's arms as the water hit the island. They were safe though as they had chosen to sit in their favourite place at the top of the mountain. They saw the waves as these crashed into the village and destroyed all in their path.

"Look at that," said Chan, "it's unbelievable what is happening, I have read of these things but I never thought that I would see such a thing."

Jo Lee cried and tried to wipe the tears from her eyes, "My family is down there."

As she watched the village, it was swept first below the waves and then when the village reappeared, houses appeared to be floating downstream. She could not hear the screams of the people, they were too far away but she imagined them.

"My family is lost!" she said.

"I will go and look for them," said Chan as he stood up.

"No, if you do that, you too may die."

"I have to go and look, my family is also there."

"Stay with me, Chan."

"I will be back soon, Jo Lee," and with these words Chan rushed down the mountain to see if anything could be done.

If only he had been a God.

As Chan rushed to help Old Nick smiled and aimed a boulder at him. As Chan rushed down the mountain, the falling boulder crushed him.

'So much for the help that you would offer other humans,' said Old Nick to himself.

"Why do you choose to do this to these mere mortals Nicky, what have they done to you that you would slake your wrath upon them?" asked The Christ as he appeared out of nowhere.

"Oh, so you want to talk to me now, Chris."

"Chan and Jo Lee are just a young couple, they are starting out their lives, why would you interrupt the flow of things?"

"Why indeed, why were you always the favoured one, that's what I want to know?"

"That does not matter, who can say what is in the mind of the All Father. What really matters is that the mortals, vulnerable as they are, are allowed to continue freely as they travel on their path of evolution. We must also ensure that we maintain a balance so as to be certain that they use their own free will to make the choices that they have to take on their own individual journeys."

"You do waffle so much sometimes Chris; bugger the mortals, is what I say, they deserve what they get."

"You are wrong Nick, look after them now and they will repay your trust in them forever."

"They have already forgotten me; they do not worship me as they do you."

"The times are changing, more and more of these humans now worship who they please, but you have to earn their trust by repaying them for their worship. Remember that without their worship, you will fade and die."

"I give them everything that they ever could wish for and more. The ones that are true to me are very happy."

"You spoil them with your gifts, spoil them like a child, and all they do is take and then they become lazy and frivolous. You must become the teacher that you once were. You must teach them about the balance. One soul cannot have everything it wants as it would outweigh all the others and become fat and bloated. Everyone deserves a slice of the cake. You must treat them with respect and gain respect in return."

"As to those that worship you, do you think that they respect you?"

"I can only hope."

"Ah, but more and more are turning to me now, more and more appreciate what I give them."

"You give them false hope, Nick; you cannot continue to give everything to everyone. At some point the hurt will set in and your worshippers will become disinterested in you and then they will turn away from you."

"Why can I not give them everything that they desire, it is within my power to do so."

"No, it is not, for every one that you shower gifts upon, another will hurt, this is the way of things. We need to share the love as well as the hurt; that is our role in the existence that we are."

"You are so wrong in your thinking, I give to my worshippers what they need and they are happy, yours just suffer all the time. One day they'll turn to me for help."

"They may turn yes, they have the free will to do that but they may return too, they have always returned to me."

"They return to you for more of the same old suffering that you have always offered. Is it any wonder that I have no respect for these humans. You talk nonsense Chris, you always did," and with these words, he faded back to where he came from.

"Oh Nick, will you never understand!"

Chris then channeled his thoughts and looked down on the mountain to see the sobbing Jo Lee. He also looked down at the place where the boulder had landed to check if his miracle had worked. Chris smiled, Chan had not died as the boulder had hit the earth because the hole that Chan had fallen into had been too low for the crashing boulder to do him any damage. The hole had been prepared by Chris himself, on the sly, to outwit Nick.

Chris smiled at this minor miracle, as did Chan, as he pushed his way out into the open.

After he had climbed up to a safe vantage point, Chan looked down at the damage below that the tsunami had caused and then sat a while as he caught his racing mind. The village was devastated. Most people were dead or missing. In this mayhem and chaos he may lose Jo too, he feared.

So it was that Chan made his way back to where Jo Lee sat. Together their faces shone on seeing each other. And as they ran to hold each other, the sun came out and shone on the land below.

Their love reached out across the universe. Some people smiled at that moment for no reason. They smiled because they felt God's presence.

MERMAID AND RADHA

୫੭

At the end of the day when nature had unleashed its wrath on her country and its people, Jo Lee sat nervous and fearful. The city was in a shambles beneath them and yet her heart was glad that Chan was by her side. Through her tears she saw a luminous light that enveloped the peak of the mountain, across the valley. Krishna was watching them over from a distance; pensive and wistful, smiling and sad, because the lovers reminded him of Radha.

Krishna, the God, had passed on to the next incarnation but Radha's love had stayed with him. Radha had loved Krishna of previous incarnation with the simple feminine love that a woman nurtures in her heart for a man. She had loved him as a man and a God.

'Only mortals can love unconditionally. Goddesses cannot surrender to a lover, at least not the way women do.'

Krishna found himself yearning for Radha's love on this day. Krishna, the God, had put away his Godly arrogance to consummate love with a simple country girl who was also another man's wife. He could have chosen to snub her peasant love, he could have ignored the advances of a married woman, but he wanted the Gods to see how love alone could transcend the barriers of social norms. How is it that God could have been a lover to a mortal woman, if it was not for her compelling love? In her surrender Radha had challenged God with the love of a mortal, a love that wants permanence and therefore must end in a tragic way.

"Do you see that light there, Chan, over there, I don't know why, but I feel sad. Should you leave me, what will I do?" Jo Lee wept again and Chan felt melancholic too.

"Blessed is he whose love is returned, but greater is the love that hears no echo," Krishna addressed the ocean from the summit of a small hill; he stood with his arms across his chest and a faraway look. Though in a monk's garb, there was no mistaking Krishna's stance and the wry-sad smile on his face.

Deep down in the Pacific Ocean there lived a mermaid who had turned pensive. She had been full of joy and love once. The world of ocean was her home, but she had made the mistake of loving a man, an earthling as they were referred to. There was a rule of the Ocean, to never love an outsider. Rejected by the man, she returned to her world of water. With years nothing changed, neither her youthful beauty nor her wounded heart.

All the creatures of the ocean had gathered under the cliff, upon which Krishna stood, to catch a glimpse of the God. They marvelled at his strong limbs and imposing persona.

His face radiated from a distance, a light seemed to emanate from his being.

"Why don't you come along too?" another mermaid asked her.

"I am disappointed in Gods, besides I have no desire to meet anyone, any more," the mermaid swam away.

"Blessed is he whose love is returned, but greater is the love that hears no echo," Krishna said aloud the second time. The ocean seemed to vibrate with his words.

The sad mermaid wept at his words because she had gone through life seeking answers to her self-imposed misery. And now to hear God's very own words, it was the answer to her miserable existence. Krishna reached out his hand from the cliff into the inky waters of the ocean. His hands became invisible tentacles of embrace, which wrapped around the mermaid. The mermaid felt a current circle around her form, and she surrendered to nature's mystic embrace.

She felt neither fear nor pain, not even the dull ache that had settled on her soul for years; she floated close to the surface, without any emotion. It felt strange to not feel anything after years of living with pain.

"Why did you take so long, Lord; why did I suffer at all?" she asked. Her tears merged into the ocean and fishes swam up to caress her tear-soaked cheeks. From the hilltop Krishna smiled at the shoal of little fishes who danced merrily around the mermaid. From a distance the fishes looked like small blinking lights beneath the surface of the dark, calm sea – the twinkling little hopes in the dark ocean of life.

Then one day, just as suddenly as he had flown in, Krishna flew out. He left for his homeland because there was something that drew him back to India. Its people were lazy, corrupt, and devious but there was something about them that did not let him abandon them. They accepted their lot without protest, not because they were complacent, but because they respected God's will. Krishna could have stayed on that island forever, but he was a God and Gods are just as much, if not more, eccentric than human beings.

The next day after tsunami Chris looked down from up above and saw that Jo Lee and Chan were now entwined.

"Oh you bad boy Chris!" said Old Nick as he reappeared. "You have just broken one of the fundamental laws of the universe and you know it too. You cannot just give life like that. The boy was dead, I saw him die, and oh Chris, you are so wrong to do this."

"He did not die as your boulder landed, I had prepared the land earlier and he was quite safe in the hole that he was lying in."

"How did you know that I would throw the boulder, the only way you could know was by interfering with time itself and in doing so you have broken the law of the universe, Chan's spirit belongs to me."

"No."

"Yes, it was I who took his life and his soul should now come before me."

"No, I exercised a little influence on the mountain, that is all. That hole may have been there, anyway, these two youngsters will live a life together and that is the end of it."

"And you talk of balance! These two have even now had more than their fair share of favouritism from you."

"The balance was interfered with but now the balance will continue as normal, I know that they have had a good deal of luck but they will have some bad luck along the road to enlightenment and the balance will be restored."

"I still say that you are wrong, you in your way are as bad as me in mine."

"Not so, look around you, Nick, just look at the mountain and tell me what you see."

Old Nick looked about the decrepit place, houses had been washed away, fishing boats capsized, people killed, bodies washed out to sea and back again, and as the bodies returned they were more bloated than when they left. Even more, people bore the scars of radiation poisoning. Fish floated wide-eyed and horrible on the foam of the sea.

"It is nothing that I have not seen before," replied the Devil.

"Look closer."

Nick looked again and then he spotted what Chris was talking about, for there in the chaos he saw Krishna walking through the disaster, trying to give as much help as he could and as he looked, he also saw the Buddha himself as he tried to bring comfort to the dead and dying. Other Gods could also be seen trying to help out as best they could, the Little Old Man, Brahma, Muhammad, Feng Pho-Pho, Bishamon, Ra and even Abora had come to help.

"Do you not see Nick, do you not understand the suffering that is coming from this place? It needs a balance and these Gods are doing their best to sort out the suffering so they can carry some of the burden themselves."

"You talk nonsense Chris, you always did," and with these words, he faded back to where he had come from.

"Oh Nick, will you never understand."

Chris looked down on the two lovers and smiled, at least these two had survived and were happy for the moment.

Time moved on and Chris went back to his Heaven. Krishna decided to board a flight back home because he had been moving around in his astral body for far too long. And so he made his way to the airport to fly back home as a mortal does.

THE RETURN OF KRISHNA

৪০

At the airlines office, a young booking clerk was even now trying to make a name for herself as she was sure that her bosses were watching her via the closed circuit TV system. This young woman was not the sort to take any sort of cheek and just wanted to be noticed so she could eventually rise high into the echelons of the company that she now worked for.

"We need to see your passport and visa, sir, before we can issue you a ticket, though we can block a seat for you at the moment. I suggest you fax or mail a scanned copy of the first and the last leaf of your passport along with the visa page, as soon as possible. Can I assist you further on this, sir?" asked this young woman, her smile crisp and artificial.

Krishna's plans of easy, leisurely travel were ruffled in the wake of this new information. He was bored of making himself vanish and then reappear at another place, and even another time. 'It must be so much easier to fly down,' he had concluded. And now as he considered the list of documents he was expected to produce, it became clear to him that only Godly intervention could bail him out. He had come to Japan without a passport or a visa, but now the authorities wouldn't allow him to leave the shores of their country until he produced concrete evidence of his identity along with a valid visa that had allowed him into their country. So Krishna went about creating a navy blue passport cover with the Ashoka emblem embossed in the centre and pale green leaves inside. He did not dither for a moment when deciding on the colour of the passport cover. He could, if he so desired, have created a passport of any country of his preference – immigration simplified.

However much he was disappointed in his country, which had at one time been a philosophically superior civilization, he could not leave it forever. And in a way, he thought, he belonged with all those who believed in him. After creating all the documents that were demanded of him, Krishna bought a flashy, lightweight, trolley suitcase that could swivel 360 degrees on its wheels. "Now this is going to be a real flying experience," he said to the saleswoman.

He awaited his first air travel with eagerness. When the day to leave for his land arrived, he called a cab to reach the airport – 'How very touristy,' he thought. 'Gods are no more than tourists on earth,' he smiled at the thought. As he got down, he wondered if he had reached a crowded, chaotic place on earth where harried men and women were running about. 'Why, this looks like a war front. Has this transport been created by man to make life easier, or is he being harassed by his own creations?' Even before the adventure could start, he was beginning to have misgivings about it.

Everybody was either headed somewhere, or screwing their eyes at the screens, or filling in some form or the other. Krishna learnt later that all the passengers were required to produce their national identity document along with the ticket, at all the gates that they passed in order to reach the aerobridge. And all those gates, barriers, counters, etc., felt like hurdles in a marathon race. Also, he found himself screening the passport repeatedly to fill out the forms. There was a passport number, the date of issue, the date of expiry, the visa category and so on and so forth that had to be filled out in the forms. Krishna had expected air travel to be like the cinemas, where people hand their ticket at the gate and are led to their seat.

'Where are the damn planes?' Krishna looked all around on entering the airport. There were rows of cubicles spread out before him in a colossal hall.

"Hello there, good man, can you tell me where the plane is that will take me to India?" Krishna asked the guard at the gate. The guard, though amused, guided him to the Help Desk, with an unflinching straight expression. A severe looking man at the Help Desk pointed him further down to aisle F, counter 5. For a change, the attractive lady at counter 5 laughed at his question.

"Good sense of humour, sir," she said. His passport and ticket were scrutinized a second time and bags once weighed, were put away on a carousel.

"I am quite fine carrying that suitcase actually; it's brand new and extremely light. I would much rather keep it with myself," Krishna protested with the woman at the airlines counter. She looked at him in disbelief. A young airlines assistant stepped in to diffuse the confusion. He was at pains to explain the check-in procedure to Krishna.

"I assure you sir, your baggage will arrive in good condition at Delhi airport. And even if it doesn't, you will be compensated by our baggage claim. Don't you worry sir, and here's the form which you must fill in and submit at the Immigration."

"Immigration! You mean I can't get into my plane yet?" The lady at the counter no longer smiled at what she thought was a poor joke.

After an interminable wait at the immigration and security-check, where his papers were re-checked for the third and then the fourth time, he was made to walk through a metal detector. No sooner had he passed through the machine than the alarm started to beep. Suddenly an airport official who had been watching the passengers walk through the detector, straightened up. As he drew himself erect, he looked even more firm and alert than before.

'What on earth was that?' Krishna felt his heart beat with such rapid force in reaction to the shrill alarm of the metal detector that he forgot he was an omnipotent God.

"Step aside, sir. Do you have coins in your pocket, or some sharp object, or a metal chain on your person, or some such thing?" the guard frisked him briskly. All through the act of frisking, the officer's expression remained fixed and devoid of emotion. Before Krishna could understand the gravity of his situation or even think out his course of action, the security officer was done with the first level of frisking. "Please take off your shoes and walk through the machine again." Krishna carried out the instructions duly; this time, to his relief, the machine remained silent.

"You may now collect your bags from the X-Ray," the officer lost whatever interest he had had in Krishna and his gaze fixed itself on the machine once again; his face drawn into a stiff expression.

"Just a minute officer, can I go back and get my shoes?" Krishna pointed to his shoes behind the metal detecting machine.

The officer's gaze shifted from Krishna's face to the well-polished shoes just behind the metal detector. His face, which had been impervious to the drama around him, now drew into an expression that was a mix of exasperation and disbelief.

"You didn't pass them through the X-Ray!"

After what had seemed like a long haul at the security, Krishna walked towards the departure lounge. 'It can't be too far,' he thought to himself. But the aircraft was still not in sight. Krishna now decided to ask his co-passengers, lest there had been a mistake on his part.

"Aircraft? Don't worry, it won't fly without you. They will call out for us when they are ready for you, be patient," the genteel old man smiled at him benevolently.

At this point Krishna was instructed to locate his gate that was to eventually lead him to the aerobridge. 'Even the gate to the Heavens is easier to find,' Krishna sighed before starting the hunt for the gate.

At the gate he smiled at all the straight-faced co-passengers. 'We are together on a journey, on this plane and even otherwise,' he thought. A couple of old women smiled back at him. Air stewards and stewardesses lined up soon after the boarding announcement. With one brisk movement barriers were drawn to segregate the privileged travellers from the unprivileged.

"We are boarding now, ladies and gentlemen. First our First Class passengers, the rest, please remain seated. The First Class please."

Everybody cleared the way for the preferred passengers and waited for their turn.

"Why always the first class?" said a displeased young boy.

"Because that guy paid hell lot of money to get on to that plane," said his grandmother with a smirk. Her face, a criss-cross of lines, was a contrast to her young, sparkling eyes.

"Thank you, ladies and gentlemen, for waiting, now we are boarding our premium economy passengers, the premium economy passengers may please proceed to the plane."

"Now, why can't we fly premium economy, grandma? It can't be all that expensive!" The boy looked straight into his grandmother's smiling green eyes. Her eyes lit up at his question.

"Don't know about that dear, but soon it will be our turn to get onto that plane. Because now they have only the cattle class left. The rest are already up there." The boy was heartbroken but when Krishna winked at him, he forgot his disappointments and beamed at all the stiff looking stewardesses.

"Last call for our premium economy and business class passengers." Everybody looked at everybody. No one moved from his position.

"Thank you for waiting, ladies and gentlemen, now we proceed to our economy passengers."

Krishna walked into the aircraft smiling at the flight crew, who though all smiles, were not smiling at anyone in particular. He had been allotted a middle seat in the side row, flanked by two old men. He squeezed his way in and sat upright to collect his thoughts. All around him there were passengers, front – behind – sides, his long legs were stuck between seats, above his head was the ceiling of the aircraft, and as far as his eyes could see there were people's legs, backs, and heads. It felt the whole mankind was closing down on him.

"Do we have to sit here, like this, for the next eight hours or more?"

The old man to his right returned a vacuous look and the one to his left replied in a terse, "Yes". Krishna looked from one man to the other and then got up.

"Ummn-I need to go, excuse me!"

All the passengers on board watched, with amusement, a man run down the aisle, while the announcement for flight take-off was in progress. The boy who was travelling with his sprightly grandmother giggled and winked at Krishna. The stewards and stewardesses started in Krishna's direction. They could not let him come in the way of their flight schedule.

"Please go back to your seat, sir. You will not be allowed back if you leave the plane now," a stewardess intercepted him.

"Sir, please, we are preparing for take-off and you are holding the passengers and the crew. I assure you we will give you a change of seat once the flight is off ground," a steward tried to negotiate with him.

"Are you in need of urgent medical attention, in which case we may hold the flight? Let me inform you, it is an offence."

The aircraft came to a halt. Krishna walked out of the aircraft amidst protests and warnings; he flung his passport into the bin at the end of the aero-bridge. As he walked out he undid his purple tie and handed it to the guard at the security-check, and off he went the way he had come - exiting from the arrivals.

In a matter of minutes, Krishna had taken off like the Gods do and within a fraction of a second he arrived at Delhi's Ramlila Grounds. He had not chosen his destination, but just wired himself to Sunderaman. And here he was now, in the middle of a protest rally.

BABA SOMDEV

༄

'What the hell is Sunderaman doing here?' Krishna whistled to himself in disbelief. He approached an agitated Sunderaman from behind, "What are you doing here, sir?"

Sunderaman fainted from shock and fell to the ground with a loud thud. Soon a *sewak* from Baba Somdev's organizational committee came to settle the matter.

"Who is this man, is he known to somebody? Poor fellow, he has been fasting along with Baba Somdev, God's child. Call the doctor from the dais, someone! Here, camera people, and all you journalists, see this! See how people are willing to die for Baba Somdev! Down with the government, down with corruption; *Baba ki jai!*"

Baba's disciples and television crews surrounded an unconscious Sunderaman. The pavilion resounded once again with slogans. Some journalists interviewed the bystanders who knew nothing of Sunderaman but they spoke nevertheless because they wanted to be on camera.

The news of Sunderaman's fainting reached Baba in a jiffy. Baba was on hunger strike at the Ramlila Grounds to protest against the corrupt practices of the Central government. Live drama of Baba's *satyagraha* and his spiritual discourse was being aired round the clock on all radio and television channels. To entertain his millions of viewers, Baba displayed *pranayam* techniques, yoga exercises, and sang *bhajans* with a team of musicians on stage. The media was skeptical of Baba's intent to agitate for the sake of people. Some newspapers called his *satyagraha* a publicity gimmick for personal ambition. Politicians lampooned his naive attempts to become a leader and challenged him to a debate on national issues. But to his die-hard followers, Baba was the leader of the poor, a messiah who had their welfare at heart.

"Come here, my child, come up on the stage, and tell us about your friend who fainted from hunger. Tell us the story of a hero – you are all heroes here, all of you who have braved the atrocities of a corrupt system! Hail the common man!"

Krishna was called onto the stage to meet Baba. Baba was surrounded by his advisory team, medical team, and some musicians. Thousands of men and women thronged the pavilion at that moment. Krishna watched them in silence. He saw his own self manifested in them all – each one of the spectators, the powerful and the commoners, the dogs, the reptiles, and the birds; they were manifestations of his Self. He closed his eyes and the entire universe became a dot within his being.

"I love you all, all of you, even the ones we raise slogans against, even the ones who have wronged us! They are ignorant; they have forgotten their true state. They cannot see themselves; they cannot connect with the truth of their existence. Let us forgive them. Let us meditate on our higher selves. Once you do that, forgiveness will follow."

All stood silent and mesmerized by Krishna's voice. Every word became one with the speaker and the speaker became their own self.

"Throw him out, he is an agent; he has been planted by our enemies. Throw them out, both him and his fat companion. He is an impostor; we have been cheated! Make sure the cameramen don't go anywhere near them," Baba whispered to his brother who, was also his business partner and a trusted confidant and, was seated next to him on the dais.

"I will handle him here, you manage him later."

Baba walked downstage to Krishna with folded hands. Then he waved to the crowds to draw attention away from the speaker.

"Well said, young man; well said! We must abhor wrong deeds, not the doer. My children, come let us pray so that our enemies learn the path of right action. Let us pray together. But before that, I request all of you who are fasting with me, to please, first assess your health. Do not perish because of me. You have your families to live for, I am a *brahmachari*; I can risk my life for the country. So my brothers, now, a round of applause for our brother here. He looks so handsome, doesn't he? What's your name, my child?"

"Krishna."

"Ah, you have taken God's name," Baba was aware of cameras zooming into his face.

"God's name, why I am the God," Krishna's words were being broadcast all over the country.

"I know you are an agent of government, oh, sorry God!" Baba fumbled under Krishna's gaze.

"Not an agent of God, Somdev, I am THE GOD!" Krishna spoke.

Krishna descended the stairs amidst cheers and slogans. Before Baba's bodyguards knew, he had vanished into the crowd. Thereafter, Baba began his sermon, which was not so much about ancient Indian philosophy as it was about the current political turmoil. It was in effect no more than an acrimonious, vituperative rally of slogans against the malpractices of the government. The slogans meant to incite his audience were losing their impact as time passed. 'We need more drama here,' the yogi thought to himself.

Sunderaman woke up to a splash of water and abuses.

"Wake up, you fat ass! You think you can fool us? Tell us who you are!"

Sunderaman had no memory of what had transpired before he fainted. He tried to assuage his persecutors by answering their questions. When his answers failed to humour them, he resorted to begging forgiveness. After a round of beating, Sunderaman passed out again. He was hungry, weary, wounded, and weak when he regained consciousness the second time.

Several years have elapsed, but on some days, when he is by himself, Sunderaman still wonders why he had been picked, beaten, and abused by Baba's men; the very Baba he had worshipped as a hero. He could never be sure if he had seen Krishna that day in the Ramlila Grounds. He can neither recall nor configure why he had fainted suddenly, or why he had been hauled up. All he remembers is the last thread of his adventure.

In the wee hours of the next morning paramilitary force had been called in by the government to vacate the grounds. Everybody, including Baba and his men, ran to escape the baton. For the next half an hour or so there was complete pandemonium. When everyone had dispersed, Sunderaman found himself free and left alone to his own designs.

'How can a virile man like me faint, what a shame! I must eat better; more nutritious food is what I need. Bloody everyone teases me at work and I go on a diet, and now I am weak! My mind is playing tricks with me, how can Krishna come here when he has been missing for months? I need sleep and I need food, yes, that's the remedy for my troubles,' Sunderaman sighed and limped barefoot out of the Ramlila Grounds. The ground was strewn with clothes, slippers, bottles, and leftover food. A stray dog was rummaging through someone's meal as a bored *hawaldar* looked at him with disinterest. Sunderaman realized how hungry he was. He remembered the warm comfort of his bed and hot filter coffee awaiting him back home. But his wallet had been confiscated by Baba's men and he was good 30 kilometres from home.

"Hey sir, can you drop me somewhere? The police attacked us this morning and I have lost everything, including my slippers." Sunderaman narrated his tale of woes to a kind scooter rider who had stopped in response to Sunderaman's desperate hand motions signaling him to stop.

"Hop on, brother!" the rider winked and pointed to the pillion seat behind, as if giving ride to strangers was the most natural thing to do.

"Thank you, sir. You know, you resemble a pantry-boy in our hospital, no kidding. Though you have a helmet on, still, there is something about you that reminds me of Krishna. But never mind, that boy ran away a long time ago." Sunderaman pinched himself to confirm he was not hallucinating again about Krishna. He sighed at the thought of last night's unwarranted ordeal he had been subjected to.

'But I know these shoulders, broad and tapering at an angle. There's no other shoulder shaped so beautifully. Hell! Why is my mind playing tricks, why can't I stop thinking of Krishna?'

ALMA MATTER, IN NICK OF TIME

৪৩

Chris sat in his study, alone now; he needed this time to contemplate on what was going on. He followed Buddha's way of meditation. So it was that with his face in his hands, he sat quietly and thought. He thought of Buddy Roy, Krishna, and Old Nick, and of what the world and the afterlife was coming to.

Old Nick, as he floated on high, feeling really hard done by, looked down from the heavens above at Frinton-on-Sea. Here he watched Alma as she walked along the beach of this contrived version of heaven. He could feel her rage as he observed her, the rage that raged within her, he could feel it, even from his lofty height.

'This one is worth a try,' he thought as he materialized behind her.

"Wonderful morning is it not?" said Nick to Alma as they walked along the beach. Alma turned and was startled for a moment. She had been an assassin while she had lived and was not used to people creeping up on her.

"Do not worry, you have not lost any of your skills, I am Chris's brother and I can creep up on even the best."

"Oh, another so-called God then," said Alma in a blasé way. "I won't believe in you either, you know."

"I could not care less whether you believe in me or not, however I can help you in your search for happiness."

"You could not possibly know what would please me," smiled Alma sardonically.

"How would you like to kill legitimated Leggy?" asked Old Nick with a smile. "How many times over would you like to kill Leggy so that your thirst for his death is finally sated?"

"It can't be done, we are both dead now and are trapped in this so-called heaven. Or so I have been told."

"Did Ati explain to you about this version of heaven? And other versions of heaven also?"

"Yes, quite plainly, he explained that I can't kill here."

"There are different heavens though. At least in my heaven you can kill as much as you like."

"I suppose that I could kill Leggy there, then?" asked Alma sarcastically, in a disbelieving manner.

"As often as you like."

"And how do I get to your so-called heaven?"

"All you have to do is to tell me that you believe in me and the deed will be done."

"What utter rubbish, I don't believe in religion, or afterlives, and least of all, you."

"Perhaps you would like a taster?"

"What do you mean by that?"

Old Nick waved his hands and before long, Alma was on a beach in another part of heaven, Jaywick.

She looked down and before her lay a switchblade as well as a .45 Colt handgun. 'How strange,' she said to herself as she picked up the weapons.

"Do you like what you see, Alma?" asked Old Nick from behind her. Alma turned swiftly and shot Nick in the chest. He fell to the ground and gasped for air as he seemed to claw to life and she bent down to listen to his final words. "You've got me Alma, now go after Leggy, he is in that building ahead of us, he is even now planning to escape from Jaywick with the biggest heist of gold that anyone has ever had." With these words, Old Nick died.

Alma smiled as she looked at Nick's crumpled body and then started walking slowly towards the building ahead with the intention of killing Legitimate Leggy one last time.

Old Nick smiled as he stood quietly by and watched Alma walk towards the building. 'I think that I may have a convert here,' he said to himself happily.

'Now for Krishna, let's see which one of his disciples I can convert next. For too long now, he and Chris have had it their own way. Now is the time for some mischief.'

Old Nick faded to nothing only to reappear in a run-down part of London. He had decided to enjoy himself on his way to Delhi and now he had taken the form of a drug dealer as he tempted a young man to take another hit of heroin. This youth had been taking drugs since he was 12 and though only 18, he appeared to be aged around 30. He was now trying to rehabilitate himself. He had been to the rehab classes and had taken minor drugs to wean himself off the harder ones.

"Just one more hit," said Nick, the drug dealer. "You have beaten the addiction once, so even if this one hit makes you crave more, you could beat it again. You are young and strong."

'One hit, should I take it, it was hard to get off the harder drugs, could I do it again?' thought the youth to himself.

"You could beat it again," said the drug dealer as if reading his mind, "just one more hit, I will even let you have this hit for half the usual price, what do you say?"

The young man smiled as he remembered the kick he got after taking heroin. Half the price was too good to resist, he readily gave in to temptation.

A few minutes later, Old Nick, who had now returned to his former likeness, approached the youth who sat on the ground in the alleyway.

"What's the problem, my friend?" he asked the youth.

"I can't seem to pick up my syringe, my fingers just go straight through it, man this is some hit that I am having," laughed the youth.

Old Nick smiled as he said, "Just you wait till the drug has worked off, you will be quite amazed at what you find then." He then faded into nothing, leaving the ghost of the dead man to wonder about his disappearance. 'Chris will have a good time with this one if he arrives in Clacton-on-Sea.'

Old Nick reappeared in Italy, this time as a TV presenter hosting an animal show. A four-year-old boy had been left on his own in a flat by his mother as she had to go out to work. She had left him a sandwich and he had a kitten to keep him company. As the boy stroked the kitten, he watched TV. The host (Old Nick) was very informative and was giving instructions on how to keep kittens clean. "You should wash them with a hand towel to keep the fleas at bay and then dry them as best you can." The young lad listened intently and decided to wash his own little kitten. And so he walked over to the kitchen sink where he then climbed onto a chair to get a hand towel. He picked it up, dowsed it in water and then went back to the kitten. He grabbed hold of it and then as it struggled he soaked it to the skin with the wet towel.

"That's the way to do it," said the host of the TV program; the lad imagined that he was being spoken to directly from the TV set. The little kitten was of course distressed and started to lick at its skin; the boy, however, had other ideas. He looked around the small room for a towel to dry the kitten with. He looked and looked but he could not find one anywhere. He then looked at the TV and noticed that the smiling presenter was now giving instructions of how some things can be dried in the microwave oven. 'What a good idea,' thought the boy, who then picked up his kitten and placed him in the oven. 'I will have him dry in no time at all.'

PING...

The TV set switched itself off as Old Nick moved onto his next destination. He was really enjoying his trip.

Up in cat heaven, Purrsey, the God of Cats, was not pleased when he met the ghost of the dead kitten and made a mental note to scratch Old Nicks' legs the next time they meet.

Nick appeared next in Greece and observed the rioting mob on the streets. This pleased him. He then saw that a woman was standing on top of a tall building and was undecided on whether to end it all. As the woman stared out into space, a figure appeared; he seemed to be standing on a pathway before her. 'I don't remember that,' she said to herelf, 'I thought that I was at the very edge.'

The figure smiled as he looked into her face and then just turned and walked off the ledge. The woman ran forward to see where he had gone and as she moved, she plummeted to her death.

Nick had of course faded and moved on by this time, only to reappear in a run-down part of Delhi. He looked at the filth and the squalor and listened to the noise of the traffic as he breathed in the petrol fumes that you could almost see. He smiled at the children walking around in rags begging. 'This is my kind of town,' he thought to himself as he threw a few coins into the air.

RAJU

৪৩

Sunderaman sat upright in his chair, with his left hand pressed against the right nostril and his right hand resting gently on the right knee, expelling air from his lungs with a loud thud. Every now and then he reached for the handkerchief on the table to clear the mucous that was emitted with expulsion of breath. Baba Somdev had simplified *pranayam*, which was otherwise to be done on the floor, in a cross-legged position. It was this flexibility that Baba had introduced in the rigid system of yoga that had won him many followers. He had tailored postures to suit fat and unfit yoga-aspirants. Sunderaman had not given up on Baba despite the fiasco at the Ramlila Grounds. He was sure there had been some misunderstanding.

Raju looked at the fat Sunderaman with wonder and then ambled into the storeroom, studying the rows of cans and rations arranged neatly on the racks. He waited, with a bored expression, for Sunderaman to resume breathing normally. As soon as Sunderaman stopped his *pranayam* exercises to enquire from Raju the purpose of his visit, Raju began to speak in a monotone.

"Three cans of fruit syrup, two vegetable stocks, and two litres of milk…"

"Where are the cooks and assistants? I am not issuing any rations to a guy who washes dishes! You go away from here and do the dishes, there are more trolleys coming in!" Sunderaman now changed his position to right hand on the left nostril. Raju did not move from his place and watched Sunderaman with a fixed gaze and unchanging expression.

"You moron! Is there some sort of circus going on here that you stand here watching, go, get back to work! You lazy, good for nothing creature – are you paid to while away your time? Shirkers all of you! The cook does not want to move his ass, he sends you down to the store, and you saunter around the place as if you are here for a morning walk." Sunderaman was piqued because he wanted to finish a hundred counts of inhales-exhales before it was time to issue the next round of rations.

"Excellent! Here you sit in your chair all day long breathing like a huge bear, and if I watch you, I am wasting my time. What are you being paid for, by the way?" Raju spoke without so much as batting an eyelid, his expression still bored and devoid of emotion.

Sunderaman knew from experience that no matter how much he fumed, Raju, with his persistence, would not budge till he had his reply. He decided to use tact to deal with this man who he suspected hid his incompetence and laziness under the pretence of being a slow-learner.

"Man, Raju, don't argue with me, I am busy. If I give you rations you will be accountable for every scrap that you pick. From now on, whoever takes something out of the store, signs this register, here look at this. So you can sign here and take what you want." Sunderaman opened a hardbound accounting register to the current page.

"Why should I sign something? I am only collecting things on their behalf. I am not falling into this signature trap; these guys are the devious sorts – I don't trust them, what if they eat it themselves and blame it on me!"

"Look man, Raju, what did I tell you the other day, keep your ass clean! I have to be fair to all of you, and at the same time I have to maintain these stock registers with utmost honesty. If I don't cover my ass, some son of a b**** will screw the accounts. It is not easy work, come let me show you." Sunderaman flipped the pages to read out a day's indent to Raju.

"I am not interested in all this paper work. Anyway, if I stay here any further you will assign me chores beyond the duty-roster. I am leaving now. I have plenty on my roster as it is." Raju still made no attempt to move, he merely shifted his gaze from his senior to the cans on the racks. Exasperated, Sunderaman gave up on completing a hundred counts of *anulom-vilom* and turned to the indent register.

"Will you make me permanent this year, sir?" Raju looked at him with an expression that demanded an answer.

"Now, is that what you have been hanging around to find out? I don't know; go and ask Mrs Desai, she decides on all this. I am a petty storekeeper with no say in any matter – these things are decided by big bosses, I only recruit temporary guys. And what's your problem? You have been a temporary worker for over six years, don't I always take you back? Now get back to work and don't annoy me with your queries." Sunderaman tried to put on an air of a benevolent supervisor, smiling between sentences, and modulating his voice to feign concern.

On every replacement against a temporary position, or the renewal of a contractual employee, Sunderaman made money through kickbacks. Mrs Desai, the chief of dietetics department, had no concrete evidence to prove his offence. She had heard stories about Sunderaman demanding bribes but with so much malice that everyone had for everyone, she could never be sure who was lying. She made no money from any deal. Also, she did her best to prevent malpractice of any sort. Though she had devised measures to check pilferage, there was only so much control that she could exercise on the working of a department with a hundred men on the rolls.

"Exactly! I have been around for six years here, why can't you make me permanent? I want my full rights as a permanent employee, everything – my medical benefits, my annual leave, and my provident fund. We are no fools, if you deserve to be a permanent employee, so do I!" Raju was in no mood to relent and Sunderaman thought of ways to avoid an altercation with this man who could cost him his job. Raju had all along resented giving a bribe for renewing his job. Whereas other pantry boys were apathetic to the whole affair of paying a certain cut from their salary to Sunderaman, after every 11 months when their case came up for renewal, Raju hated to part with his hard-earned money. Other boys accepted bribing as the way of the corrupt world to which they had become accustomed. It was a world where law was for the books and every favour could be bought – the richer you were, the easier it was to manipulate others.

"What is permanent here? You, me, this hospital, this earth? Even this earth is going to end one day. Earthquakes and tsunamis will end everything! Didn't you see what became of Japan after a tsunami? So why do you bother about a mere job, my friend?" Krishna appeared from nowhere.

For the next five minutes nothing moved in that storeroom, no one so much as batted an eyelid, and after what seemed like a long time, Raju and Sunderaman collected their wits and said, "Where the hell did you come from?"

Krishna pulled up Raju's dropped jaw and smiled at his old friends.

"Aren't you two going to greet me, I have returned after months, don't I deserve a reception?" Krishna walked around the room and then stopped in the middle of the storeroom to address his audience.

"I am back! Let me know if there is a place for me on your staff or even in your hearts, friends! If not, then I can always try at the canteen, or maybe I should go for *dharnas*."

Raju's interest was roused at the mention of alternate employment opportunities.

"This sounds good brother, take me along. What do you reckon is the going rate there? I have heard there is easy money at these rallies; all you have to do is raise slogans at the venue or participate in a protest march. I am willing to invest in a white *kurta-pyjama* if that will improve my chances at finding employment. Between you and me, I am tired of piling dishes in a dish-washer. I can no longer put up with this fat bully or those whimsical women officers! Brother, is that what you did all these months that you went missing?" By now Raju had one arm around Krishna's shoulders and the other circled around his waist.

"Hey wait! Stop! I think I saw you at Baba Somdev's rally; now don't lie to me. Were you there or not? I have a feeling I was beaten up because of you." Sunderaman came from behind and stood between the two men. Raju barely shifted a few inches to allow Sunderaman to squeeze in between them.

"Why can't you stand on the other side? Why must you always throw your weight around?" Raju protested.

"Shut up you moron! Now you, Krishna, tell me, were you there at the rally? Or maybe wait, were you driving a scooter that day?" Sunderaman searched Krishna's face for an answer, not sure where he had seen him, at the rally, or was he the jovial man who had driven him back home?

Krishna disengaged himself from Sunderaman's hold and turned to face him, "I was there everywhere; do you think I leave you, ever?"

Krishna was gone just as suddenly as he had come.

"Why did he leave? And what did he come back here for?"

****

Yashoda looked at her son with anguish and worry as he lay on the bed.

"Do you ever sleep Krishna? I am your mother and I have never seen you rest. Even as an infant you didn't sleep much." Yashoda looked at her son with sad fondness. She felt sorry that life had given him so little and yet she was happy for having him in her life.

'At least I have given him more than my parents gave me,' she murmured a prayer and blessed her son with abundance.

"Do you think your prayers can get me a Mercedes?" Krishna mocked her every time he caught her brooding in silence or staring grimly at nothing in particular.

"Think about it *Ma*, there are a billion people praying, or posting requests at the same time, God cannot be there for everyone, be reasonable." Krishna smiled at his own idol in his mother's temple.

There he stood, cast in white marble, one leg crossing over the other, with a flute to his lips. His mother had adorned the idol of God Krishna with hand-stitched silk robes. She painted the forehead of the statue with a small dot of red vermilion paste at the end of her daily prayers. The robes were changed every fortnight on the day of the full moon night. Fresh flowers were plucked every morning to offer at his feet.

"Why should you deck the Gods up every day? He will not abide by you simply because you adorn his idol so fervently!" Krishna jeered at her from his bed.

"But he has always been there for me. And the day you really need him, he will be there for you as well." She had unflinching faith in her own belief and her son's banter did not make her dubious.

Yashoda's faith in Krishna, the God as she understood, had been so deep and unflinching that when it came to finding herself a new identity, she became God's own mother. Yashoda was the name that she had found most appropriate for herself after Krishna's birth; it justified Krishna's name and her own role as a mother. She wanted to believe, for no reason in particular, that her son was not an ordinary child, and that there was something magical about his being. It was at this juncture in her life that she had turned to Krishna, the God, in complete surrender. She had refused to rejoin Sheh's brothel, which was, if you looked at it rationally, her only recourse because she was not trained for any other vocation except prostitution. Besides, she had had a fair amount of success in her profession, and for that reason everyone viewed her decision to abandon a lucrative career, in the prime of her life, unfavourably. But Yashoda was overcome with such notions of grandeur and purity after conceiving Krishna, that a life lacking in piety became abominable to her. In erasing her name, she had metaphorically annihilated Laila, the call girl, and become the legendary mother of Lord Krishna. Much like the instance when at the age of 17 her real name and identity had been erased by the pimp who had bought her from her parents.

Krishna's biological father was at one time a regular client at Sheh's brothel with a special preference for Laila. Mistaking a customer's preference for love, young Laila violated the foremost rule at Sheh's brothel. The rules had been drafted to suit the brothel's interest, which ultimately served the larger interest of the girls, their clients, clients' families, and the society. The girls were made to understand that unprotected sex was dangerous not only for their health, but also for Sheh's reputation, and finally it affected the business of the brothel. But Yashoda was young and desperately in love with a man who had nothing but lust in his heart for women. At the end of a steamy affair, she was left alone with an infant, and not a soul by her side. Sheh, the pimp and the master of the brothel, extended a helping hand by accepting her back, but she had made up her mind on creating a new and honourable life for herself and her son.

"What's that noise? Should we not go out and check?" Krishna found the nearest shirt at hand. He fumbled with buttons as the voices drew close to their house and then went past their hearing range.

"I don't think you should bother – it can't be anything more than a domestic quarrel," Yashoda peeped from the door to validate her statement.

"Oh there, what did I say? There is nothing that you can do here; this has been going on for six months. It's the room 16 couple; they involve the whole world in their quarrels. Every few weeks the wife calls in the police only to withdraw the case the very next day. Good for nothing, both the wife and the husband." Yashoda went back to Krishna, the God, and resumed the hymn that praised Lord Krishna's arrival on earth. Krishna, the son, slipped out quietly to get some fresh air.

There were no windows in their three-by-three metre room. To the right of the entrance was the kitchen adjoined to the room which was all that was there to the house. The kitchen was a small wing of the single room. There was a small bathroom with just enough space for one man and one bucket. For ventilation there was a small vent under the roof of the kitchen. The vent was the only inlet for fresh air and sunlight in the room. Smoke rose from the incense sticks, filling the room with floral aroma and smoke. Yashoda continued with her prayers unmindful of the smoke and heat.

"Is their drama over?" Yashoda looked up from her hymn book to enquire.

"How did you know I was gone? *Ma*, you know what, you don't concentrate on your Krishna," Krishna tried to parry her question.

"Maybe you are right, son, I love you too much to abandon myself to God's service. And you don't help me by disappearing for months. Where do you go, Krishna? You can at least tell me." She knew her implorations and pleas were of no avail and that she had to accept the streak of detachment in her son. Her greatest solace was that he always returned home.

"Now don't start again, *Ma*! So, are you through with your ritual or should I make myself some breakfast? You said you will make *pooris* today, remember?"

"So you are not going to answer me, now? Why don't you go out for a bit, it gets suffocating with smoke and all." She proceeded to wind up her prayers and finally drew the curtain in the temple.

"I am all right, if you can stand the smoke, then so can I. We should look for better accommodation, but as soon as I have a job I will install an exhaust fan in the kitchen." Krishna opened the main door and the sounds of the neighbourhood filled the room.

"I thought you said the damn thing was settled!" Yashoda resisted the impulse to go out.

"Why are you perturbed every time these fools fight? They are each other's victim and persecutor; they will continue to suffer together. Let's examine it rationally – the man picks a whore for the night and gets her home because he cannot afford a room in a hotel, and his wife protests, which is only a natural reaction. The altercation builds up into a big fight, next the neighbours intervene and call the police. The cops make a note of it in the daily diary, because the complaint is not serious enough to be recorded as an FIR, it's another thing that even getting an FIR lodged is a big deal in this country. But nothing gets resolved, the man and his wife continue to remain married, the whore goes back to work again, neighbours get some more gossip, the policeman gets some petty cash, end of the story. Now let's get back to our breakfast – shall we?"

"You are too young or perhaps too much of a man to understand a woman's point of view! Everyone wants to restore the higher moral order – they would rather see a man live unhappily with his wife than be happy with a prostitute – the greatest good of the greatest number! So everyone gets around to having a pound of our flesh – the clients, the pimps, the police, and finally the ministers."

Krishna watched the lines around her eyes and mouth draw into a criss-cross pattern. Never before had she alluded to her past even indirectly but today there was a slip.

"Our--no--not our, err, I meant women – yes, that's what our meant, women." Yashoda scurried into the kitchen to avoid her son's gaze. His eyes always searched for answers, reading it in others' eyes when they avoided him, never letting them hide behind false emotions.

"It's all right, I understand. You have come a long way from there, it's your past. Be assured that no man can wrong another and live in peace."

Krishna left her alone to weep in peace and recoil into her shell of memories.

When he returned home later that night, they sat a long time in silence – she knew that he knew and that he had known it for a long time.

NICK'S SPELL

൭

O ld Nick appeared in the hospital in Delhi and looked around. He made himself appear as a doctor with a white coat and stethoscope, and stood as a handsome, lean, six-footer.

Old Nick watched from outside time as Sunderaman shouted out his orders to those he considered were of a lower class than him. 'Oh I like this one,' thought Nick.

He changed to his torn jeans and 'I Rock The World' T-shirt before appearing outside Sunderaman's office.

"Hello chap," shouted Nick with verve as he walked into the office. "Any chance of some *chai*?"

Sunderaman looked up and was appalled at the gall of the youth before him. "Who the hell do you think you are; coming in here and making demands on me?" asked the fat one.

"Why, I am Dr. Nick," said Old Nick in a quiet voice, "I have heard so much about you, you know, such good reports. I thought that I would like to come and meet you and introduce myself."

"Doctor, my ass! Where's your stethoscope, doctor? And for your information this is not a doctors' mess, this kitchen is meant for the patients in the hospital."

"Oh I have only just arrived today, besides I don't carry stethoscope around everywhere. You look like an old hand yourself though. I am sure that you recognize a proper doctor when you see one."

Sunderaman though looked suspicious, "Who has told you about me *eh*?"

"Why, my brother Krishna, he has told me so much about you, you should be pleased at what he has told me."

"Krishna? You think you can bluff me, he is just a low caste son of a whore! And from what I know that woman has only one son."

"I am the legitimate son of his father; even though my father didn't own him up, to me he is a brother," Nick replied, looking solemn and grave.

"Well, you certainly resemble him; though that sister f***** is a bit of a mischief maker. You look decent enough though. I suppose being legitimate has its advantages, but you see you will not get far here unless you act like a doctor, and never ever mention that Krishna is a relation. I suppose I will have to take you under my wing," said Sunderaman, slyly.

"I suppose that you will, I am feeling quite lost here. You seem more in control and *er-* let's say cultivated," replied Nick as he sowed his seeds of mischief.

"After all," said the fat Sunderaman, "you were born from a man who did prostitutes! So you are at a disadvantage, and you had better know it. I come from a Brahmin family, here we don't have much sex even with our wives, all those days of observing fasts and penance, you know. We are not like, don't mind *haan*, all those bastards who must screw every night before they sleep."

"Oh, I know my place and I also know yours. You do not look well at all, a little worried and harassed or maybe you have blood pressure?" asked the smiling Nick.

"Who do you think that you are? You come in here pretending to be a doctor. I am very well and you keep that blood pressure thing to yourself. It is your brother and that moron Raju who are threatening to blow the whistle on me. They think they can complain about me, or arm-twist me into giving them a permanent post; they are mistaken. Don't imagine I trust you any more than I trust him, you sons of a f****** ass! Tell him to keep off me. How dare he mess with me? As for you, you don't even look half as intelligent as our pantry boys; do you expect me to believe you are a doctor?"

Old Nick smiled at Sunderaman.

"Why do you smile at me, you f*****, I can have you thrown out of this building any time that I want to."

Nick, with a flick of his thumb, produced a briefcase on the table, and after opening it removed a white coat and a stethoscope.

"You are no doctor, you f*****, I can sense it," said Sunderaman.

"You have me there, friend Sunderaman, I am not a registered doctor, but I can heal with magic."

"Magic! Have you run away from a mental asylum? You think I am going to believe this shit!"

"Believe or not, I have come here just to help you, my friend."

"Help me? and what makes you think that I need any help anyway?" laughed the distrusting Sunderaman.

"Oh you need my help, my friend, look at you, you are overweight and if you do not lose some weight soon then you will die. I can make you healthy again. You also crave wealth; I can help you gain it. But most of all, friend Sunderaman, most of all, you wish to have the nurse called Shiny, I can help you there too."

"Ho, ho, ho, don't give me that crap! Do I look like a gullible idiot to you?"

Old Nick smiled once again and as he did, the door to the office shut with a thud and the room seemed to grow bigger.

"What the f*** is going on?" asked Sunderaman.

"Be quiet, you fool, it is settling down now," and indeed the room stopped growing; it seemed to Sunderaman that they were now in a colossal hall. Baskets laden with golden trinkets and jewels were spread on the tables in the centre of the hall.

"What has happened, where are we?" asked Sunderaman.

"We are in my place, in my time. Look around you, my friend; you can have whatever you want from this room. Just help yourself and after you have decided what you want to take back to your office, just look at yourself in that mirror over there."

Sunderaman looked at the jewels and the golden trinkets and began to stuff random things into his pockets. When he had stuffed his pockets and no more would fit in, he filled a bag with even more jewels. He then walked over to the mirror as he had been told to do. As he looked at the reflection, he was amazed at the figure that stared back at him. It was as if he had been taken back in time by 20 years, for there in the mirror was the young man that he had once been.

"What trickery is this, you f*****, why do you torture me like this, it is not real and neither are these trinkets that you have given me," and as he said these words, he swore some more, while slinging the gold and jewels to one side.

"Quite a shock is it not, friend Sunderaman? But this is how I can make you look if you want, and the gold and jewellery are quite real. But look once again into the mirror, for this can also show you what else can happen if you only pledge your loyalty to me."

Sunderaman looked once again into the mirror and this time it became a sort of window and as he looked, he saw a bedroom. The bed within it was plush with silk cushions and satin leopard-print linen and on the bed lay nurse Shiny. She was quite naked and quite beautiful. Sunderaman's mouth started to drool as he thought of the things he could have done to this woman had he only been younger, but as he watched he saw his younger self approach the bed. He watched for some time as his younger self then went on to pleasure himself with the young nurse.

"This is not real, it can't be. Why torture me so, you f*****!"

"It can be real, Sunderaman. I can make it real; all you have to do is to believe in me."

"You talk as if you are some kind of God then."

"I am indeed a God."

"Not one that I have heard of, and look at you, you are the wrong colour to be any kind of God. Remember I am the son of a Brahmin and I know more about Gods than a layman. I may not know all the 33,000 Gods, but I recognize all the important ones. To me you look like a hippy, the grass-smoking ones who lodge in Paharganj inns!"

Old Nick smiled as he looked at the worried Sunderaman, "I am a God of the Christian faith, Sunderaman, and not all Gods are of the Hindu religion."

"What nonsense you talk, you are no God; why if you were a God then that would mean that your brother Krishna is also a God?"

"He is, I am, and we both are. You can have what you want if you side with me. For too long now has Krishna walked this Earth in piety! It is time for me to have some fun. Come join me Sunderaman, and you will enjoy yourself for eternity."

"This is too much for me," cried a shaking Sunderaman, "I am getting dizzy," and as he spoke, he fainted.

Sometime later he awoke as he sat on his chair in his office.

'That was some dream,' he said to himself as he took a sip of water from the golden chalice on his desk. He never really noticed the goblet though and just walked over to the sink to splash some water over his face. He turned on the tap as he splashed water on his face, he looked at his reflection in the mirror. There, looking back at him, was the face that had been his, some 20 years before.

THE PATH OF BUDDHA

ꕥ

As Christ sat in quiet contemplation, he somehow knew that he had just received a message on his Facebook account. So he moved his mouse and the screen suddenly appeared before him. The message read:

Why so sad, young Chris, we are all here for just a second in the eye of eternity, smile my lad or you may start to get frown lines on your forehead.

Chris smiled at once. Buddha had a way of lifting his spirit.

"Hello Buddy Roy," he wrote back, "I am just following your advice and meditating on the whole existence thing."

"And what conclusions have you drawn?"

"None really but my headache seems to have cleared slightly."

"You are worrying about Old Nick too much, my boy."

"But he causes chaos wherever he goes, why does he have to make everything so complicated?"

"Would you have it any other way, would you be happy to walk through the whole of existence with everything happening correctly? Where would the challenge be in that? Even eternity can become stale."

"How can eternity become stale? There is so much to see, so much to do, so many people and spirits and even Gods to meet."

"Yes, you are almost there now, you are correct to a degree in what you say, but impermanence is the only truth. Nick, the Devil, and all those destructive forces only go to prove that nothing will remain the same. These Gods remind us of the ongoing eternal change. Would you have everything the same? As a God you must remember to not attach yourself to anything at all, just let the world pass through this storm. Once man follows the path of *nirvana*, he will be liberated from the cycle of sorrow and happiness."

"You are wise beyond words," typed Chris, "but I still worry."

"It is natural for you to worry, you would be the wrong God for the job that you are doing, if you didn't. As would Old Nick be, in the wrong job, if he did not cause the chaos that he does every now and then."

"I suppose you are right, I just needed some time on my own to think a little."

"Meditation is good for the soul and the mind, but there is work to be done. Even now Old Nick is weaving a web that will come to test your patience. Although, you may come to thank him for some of what is about to happen."

As Chris looked at the computer screen, he saw that Buddy Roy had now logged off. 'How strange you are sometimes Roy.' But already, in his mind, Chris knew that Old Nick was planning something. 'Something is happening now,' thought Chris as he disappeared to search the heavens and to see what was going on.

The Buddha floated a foot above the ground as he had watched the keyboard as it had typed what he had wanted it to type. 'How strange this modern technology,' he thought. He then faded from where he was and reappeared on the coast of India, and then to a little place called Mahabalipuram. This was one of his favourite places. Here he could soak up the sun and meditate while he breathed in the sea air. The Buddha at least was at one with himself.

LEGGY AND ALMA

୫୬

Alma cocked her gun slowly and silently as she walked towards the big warehouse. In here, she had been told, was Legitimate Leggy. She opened the door to the warehouse slowly so the door would not creak. She sidled her way through the crates that occupied the shadows within. As her eyes grew accustomed to the dark, she saw Leggy ahead of her; he was counting and numbering the gold bars that he placed in the crate before him.

'I have you now, you bastard, at long last, there will be reckoning,' the lady thought to herself.

Alma took aim and squeezed the trigger and as the gun fired out the bullet, Legitimate Leggy fell to the ground. Alma ran forward and as he lay on the ground in agony, she stood above him and said, "I don't know whether to put another bullet into you and end your life or whether I should just watch as you die in agony."

Leggy returned her stare and smiled, "Why, Alma, why?"

"Why? Because you ruined my life. Why? Because I can," and with these words, she shot Leggy in the forehead and he died before her. He then disappeared.

Alma too disappeared and once again stood outside the warehouse. This time she walked over to it and yanked open the door loudly.

"Leggy, I have come for you!" she shouted.

Leggy, seeing her enter the warehouse, dropped the bar of gold that he had been holding and went for his gun. He fired at Alma but the bullet whizzed past her ear into a crate.

"Unlucky Leggy," shouted Alma, "you missed but I am not going to." She then crept round behind him and saw him positioned behind a crate as he looked for her. Alma took careful aim and shot Leggy in the leg. He fell to the ground but as he fell, he let off a shot that only barely missed her.

"Good try Leggy," cried Alma excitedly. She then took a careful aim and again fired a shot. This time it hit him in the left shoulder.

Leggy screamed with pain and shouted out to her as best he could. "Alma, I have enough gold here for both of us, let me live and we can be rich together."

"F*** you!" shouted Alma as she again squeezed the trigger that sent a bullet soaring forward. This time the bullet hit Leggy between the eyes and he then crumpled down dead once more. Alma was really enjoying herself.

Again she materialized outside the warehouse and then crept up to the door. This time she decided to climb up to a window and take Leggy's life from above. She entered from the second-storey window and as she looked down she saw that Leggy was counting and numbering his gold. 'I have you now,' she said to herself softly as she let off a shot from her gun. Leggy was hit in the stomach and his gun went flying across the floor.

"This time I am going to kill you slowly," said Alma to the figure on the floor as she produced her cut throat razor.

She was about to kneel down and do the deed when she noticed a change in the features of the body that lay before her. His whole physiology seemed to change and as she looked, she also heard these words spoken to her by the new figure that now rose from the floor.

"Do you wish to cut my throat open, Alma? Is this what you want, will it really satisfy you? Will it satisfy your hatred?" asked the Christ as he appeared.

"What is this, where is Legitimate Leggy, I was told that I could kill him over and over and now you appear to ruin it all."

"Alma, think, use your intelligence. You killed him when he lived and he killed you and now you are both dead and here in heaven. There is no death here, wake up and smell the roses."

"But I was promised, Nick swore to me that if I believed in him, then I could kill Leggy again."

"It is not real Alma, this place. This place is just a figment of your imagination. That's right, *your imagination*. Old Nick is a clever God and he has worked his wonder on you. Yes you can kill Leggy here but it is just imaginative, that's all. It is not real, he is playing with you. All he wants is your soul. He laughs as you try again to kill your enemy. You still have a choice, Alma. You can choose to stay here and kill Legitimate Leggy as many times and in as many ways as you want or you can choose to come back to the Heavenly Frinton-on-Sea with me and you can begin a new life. What is it to be?"

Alma looked at the fading body of Legitimate Leggy and then burst into tears. "I have hated him so much I just wanted to kill him again. He spoilt my life, you know, and I wanted revenge."

"I think that you have had your fun Alma, you have killed him more often than he deserved."

"He is not really dead though, is he?"

"Of course he is dead, as dead as any of the spirits that dwell here in this heaven."

"What shall I do then? I cannot stop hating him, I cannot kill him, either?"

"Come back to heaven with me, the job of the Ati will be advertised again soon and I feel that you would be a prime candidate. You will have no time to hate once you are on the job."

"What of Nick though? I have told him that I will believe in him."

"Did you sign a contract?" asked Chris, "one that was written in blood."

"Well no, he just said that I should try this for a while."

"Try before you buy, Nick is indeed a modern God. Well then you have nothing to worry about and it looks like we will soon have a passionate Ati on board."

Chris guided the spirit of Alma back to Frinton and then asked her what she wanted to do next.

"I am going to have a bath, and then I am going to go over to the café and have breakfast with Legitimate Leggy. I think that it is time that we had a talk and let bygones be bygones."

Chris smiled at this and walked off to his little cottage by the sea. Something was still niggling at the back of his mind, though.

THE MAGICAL SPELL

๙

Sunderaman, this big bag of flesh that he was, kept looking at himself in the mirror and it was nothing short of a wonder. He was no longer the big heap of flesh that he had become after years of a wasted and abusive life. He was now once again his youthful self. Sunderaman smiled at his reflection and this smile grew even bigger as he noticed that he had a full set of teeth, even, clean, sparkling white teeth with not a touch of yellow upon them. He looked at his lean body and smiled some more. 'Youth is wasted on the young,' he thought, 'but now I get to have a second go at it.'

Sunderaman started to sing and dance as he became aware of his fresh, healthy body and felt a surge of excitement recalling the days of his youth. The radio played a Tamil film song and Sunderaman imagined that he now looked no less than the Tamil cine-superstar, Rajnikanth; with that thought he felt happier and turned up the volume. Nick watched him dance from his space and time and convinced that he had found his man, he set about to reward him.

"What is all this noise, Sunderaman, why do you dance so, have you taken leave of your senses?" Shiny stood right in front of him, alone, in his office.

"Oh what a pleasant surprise; so you heard about the miracle? Now, what do you say to this, my sweet little pudding?" Sunderaman stood up to his full length and exhibited himself to impress the lady with his appearance.

"Pudding, my foot! All you can think of is food and why are you behaving so strangely? I suspect you have lost your mind!"

"Now come on, say it, tell me that I am handsome, tell me how sexy I look, see how firm and youthful my body is!" Sunderaman turned around to flaunt, what he imagined, was his supple, taut and well-built body.

"You are mad, quite mad, you have not changed since the day I first saw you."

Sunderaman looked at the nurse. "You find me handsome then?" he asked.

"Find you handsome, you must be kidding yourself! You are a middle-aged, married uncle, you are fat, and you are not even educated! I will never look at you, not even if you were the last man on this earth! Now turn off that radio, we can hear you right down in the ward! And next time you talk rubbish I will report you to the authorities!"

"I know why you are jumping so much – it's because of that new doctor, mind my words, he will f*** you and leave you with a bloated belly. These doctors think nothing of you nurses; to them you girls are no more than an amusement. He will use and discard you, and then you will have nowhere to go!"

"Just shut up and mind your own business! What I do with my life is my business, you keep out of it!" She was seething as she spoke because somewhere Sunderaman's words, though spoken with the pain of rejection, had a ring of truth.

Even Sister Joana, the spinster nurse, had put in a word of caution. "My girl, don't ever get involved with these dogs! That's what these resident doctors are, at least to us."

Shiny reminded herself of her lover's embrace and their moments of intimacy when he had professed his undying love for her. She left the room with a heart full of fear.

'I will have you yet, Sister Shiny,' thought Sunderaman to himself. He then walked over to the chest that had been placed next to his table and on opening it, he looked and smiled at all the gems and gold that it contained.

'Oh yes, I will have you Shiny, you and your doctor friend.'

YASHODA'S FALL

℘

Not too far from the hospital, the International Krishna temple was gearing up for *Janmashthmi* – young volunteers were busy carrying out the orders they had been given a month in advance. They had a detailed account of daily duties, running up to the day after *Janmashthmi.* The volunteers, mostly young men in their twenties or less, were either driven by their faith in Krishna or a lack of purpose in their own lives. The managing committee of the Foundation, to which the temple was attached, used them for everything from managing queues of devotees outside the temple on auspicious days, to sweeping the floors, to distributing flyers and books published by the foundation at traffic lights, and in any way the Foundation could use them to further its interest. These young volunteers were posted, by rotation, to temples all over the world; and all this they did, of free volition, in exchange for little or no remuneration.

Yashoda made an annual trip, around the occasion of *Janmashthmi* festival, to the Krishna temple as a mark of obeisance to her Lord Krishna. This year she had come three weeks prior to *Janmashthmi* in order to avoid long queues. As she did the *parikarma*, she noticed a young, tall and handsome volunteer looking in her direction. His smile seemed to say, 'At last we meet.' She found herself returning his smile. Unsure of what to make of a stranger's smile, she looked away. When she turned behind after a minute he was gone. It was not uncommon to see young men of foreign origin in the temple around *Janmashthmi.*

128

Devotees were being hurried with their prayers that day because of an unexpected heavy rush and also for security reasons. Armed policemen and paramilitary forces had been deployed to guard the temple precincts against a possible terrorist attack. There were raised barricades around the temple for better vigilance and surveillance cameras had also been installed everywhere. But all this did not come in the way of celebrations and festive spirit.

Devotees complained to no one in particular about how convenient it was, till ten years back when there were no barricades and security cordons to negotiate; but it was all said in good humour and jest. Festive spirit made people smile at strangers. Yashoda, inspired by the sentiment of the place, walked with light steps to collect her shoes from the shoe-deposit counter.

"Here, mother, are these your slippers?" the young foreigner handed her the slippers from behind the counter. His smile was beatific and warm, like that of a young boy who had found a lost toy.

"Why, yes! How did you guess? I haven't handed in my counter-token as yet, here keep this, son," Yashoda fumbled for the token in her bag. The token had been handed to her at the shoe counter upon depositing her slippers before entering the main temple arena.

"This is all that I wanted to hear you say, you cannot imagine how much it means to me. I volunteered in the temple to meet you. I have waited all these days, here, to see you. My father was so right in saying that you are the kindest soul on earth." He spoke to her with folded hands and his eyes fixed to the ground. She withdrew her feet under the sari to hide cracked heels, awkwardly shifting weight from one foot to the other.

'Who is he? How does he know me and my slippers? And who is his father?' She struggled to resolve the riddle in her mind. 'He is either an old acquaintance or he has mistaken me for someone else.'

Yashoda worked all the probable combinations as she slipped her feet into her slippers and proceeded to the nearby tap to wash her hands. All the while, she tried to summon courage to probe the stranger about his whereabouts. 'After all he is only a young boy,' she reasoned with herself.

"I hope I did not shock you with my abrupt arrival?" The young man now stood by her side.

"Who are you?" she asked him directly.

"You don't trust me, do you, Yashoda *ma*? You are afraid that I will rake up your past? I am no different from Krishna, I am like a son to you. Krishna is my half-brother, mother."

"You are? Oh my God, are you his son?" Before she could assimilate the development and fully understand the import of his words, he lay prostrate on the ground before her. His hands touched her toes gently in reverence. She cringed in horror to disassociate herself from the reminder of her past.

"What business do you have coming after me? Why do you seek me out when your father had abandoned us? Why come here and make a mockery of our status? I live happily with my son; please don't cross paths with us. I know your father died last year; on whose behest do you come to me then? You don't even look like him or any of us!" She was reminded of the humiliation she had borne in the past, of how she had been kicked when she had pleaded for succour, and of how life had meted out nothing but shame on her.

Nick had anticipated that to trick an illiterate, simple woman would be quick and easy. Some cajoling and display of sentimentality would sway her in his favour. But here he was prostrate on the ground and she had not so much as relented. As he rose to his feet, he ran over the argument he could present to impress her. 'Sunderaman had been so much easier,' he thought.

"Don't let the hatred for my father sully things between us. I am just as much his son as Krishna. He was neither faithful nor kind to my mother, who died long before him. I am alone in this world; therefore I seek you and my brother. If you despise me because of your past hurt, which I did not bring about, then I have no recourse but to accept your wish." He joined his palms in salute and walked away, appearing dejected and sad, to where she had first sighted him.

Some moments have a greater bearing on our life than others; some moments are more decisive; they are more powerful than other moments. Yashoda was to learn later the significance of this moment in her life.

She called out, "Wait a minute, son."

Sometime later, as they sat in her room, Yashoda asked him, "Why have you come here? I have no wealth to give, nor has Krishna. We are quite poor and just about make our way through this life."

"I have nothing either, mother, I am as poor as both of you but I have found myself wandering. And with nowhere to go, it was a natural progression to seek out my brother and you, the mother of my father's son."

Yashoda poured tea into the cups that were on the table. "Here drink this tea, they are reused leaves but they still have taste."

Old Nick sipped and said, "It is the best *chai* that I have tasted for a while and that's the truth."

"What will you say to Krishna when you meet him?" asked Yashoda. "I have never spoken to him about your father or my past. He will feel let down, oh it's not so simple!"

"You are so gullible, mother," replied Nick, "he has known all along, it's only to save you shame and humiliation that he feigns ignorance. As for me, he will accept me provided I have your support. You do believe in me mother, don't you?"

Time moved on and the world with it.

YOUNG BILLY

೮೦

Chris looked at the youth who sat on the beach before him. The lad looked older than his 18 years and appeared to be talking to himself. Chris listened for a moment or two.

'Where am I? I only took one hit. I should be in London. Why am I sitting here on this beach? What will mother think when she realises that I am dead? For I am dead, surely, because everything has changed. Surely this is no dream; it is certainly not like any hit that I have taken in the past. I was doing so well, why did I have to do pusher, why did I take that last hit?'

"Hello," said Chris as he looked at the youth's back. The youth turned and Chris noticed that he had been crying. "Why so sad, young Billy?" he inquired.

"Where am I?" asked Billy.

"You are sitting on a beach, my friend, the air is warm and cool and so are we. So why so sad?"

"Am I dead?"

"Why do you ask?"

The youth then went on to explain not only his recent life but also his recent death.

"I am sorry to say that your life as you knew it is now over but it is pleasant here and you will enjoy yourself from now on."

"Are there drugs here? Drugs to make me happy?" asked the youth.

"Not as such but you will learn that here, we all live on a natural high."

"That remains to be seen, lord."

Chris took the youth off to the welcoming centre and asked Alma to go easy on him as she explained what would happen to him. He then thought to himself about what he had been told by young Billy.

'What are you up to Nick, what are you going to spring on me next, and why?'

As he walked along the beach back to his cottage, he noticed that Purrsey, the God of Cats, was sitting on a rock chewing on a fish. "Hi, Purrsey, how goes it?"

"Not well," mewed the cat as he told Chris of what had happened. Chris tried to keep his calm by taking a deep breath. Further down he met the woman who had been encouraged by Nick to jump off the high building. His temper started to get the better of him. And then as he walked on, he bumped into the woman doctor who had thrown herself in front of a train.

"Enough," he shouted, "I won't allow you to have your way, now. Watch out Old Nick, I am coming." And as he said these words, he faded into nothing. It was left to Alma to welcome the new souls.

In another part of the world, Krishna walked through the dingy streets of the forgotten, dark alleys of Old Delhi; he was now reflecting on the new developments in his own world. He sat in silent repose, weary of all that was going around him; his mother's new-found love for her lover's son was a projection of her erstwhile love, a love that she had not forgotten. She, who had declared her lover despicable and avowed to never look at him again; she, the Kali of a woman, should now shower affection on her ex-lover's son. She wanted to re-construct a bond that never was. That she, whom Krishna, the God, had chosen for a mother, should have faltered; this and other thoughts had vexed him all day. He sat in silence, meditating, and still.

'Are we any different then?' asked the Buddha at the back of his mind.

'We seldom falter, Roy. We forgive man more than he forgives us. We overlook his shortcomings ever so often. But when we choose men and women for our earthly parents, they have to rise above their petty selves. They have to be God-like if not Gods,' Krishna talked to himself and the Buddha in his mind smiled. 'No Krishna, we let them down too. They forgive us as much as we forgive them.'

'I fear you believe in man more than you do in Gods, Buddy Roy!' replied Krishna to himself as he watched the rickshaw-puller draw to the kerb. The man on the back seat got off the rickshaw, limping. He cursed Lord Krishna for his arthritic woes.

"Have you not had your fill of vindictive pleasure, Krishna? When will you stop! Do you want to see me crippled, you wicked God!" The man spat with much force and anger. His spit missed Krihsna by a fraction of an inch. Krishna found his humour return. Krishna chuckled to himself as he resumed his walk. 'Gods do make man's life miserable,' he thought.

'People like your mother worship us, they pray to us. If we were not here then they would have nothing to hold on to, they are not infallible, forgive them and remember that we are not above reproach.' Buddha escorted him in his walk.

'I suppose we have never been above reproach, but never before did men curse us the way they do now. Did you not see that man on the rickshaw, that fat hulk was riding on a poor man's back! He should be walking with those knees. Now, when his knees fail to get him off a rickshaw, he curses Gods! What can we expect of these ungrateful mortals?'

Buddha thought for a moment and then replied, 'They are young souls, Krishna. Don't blame them, show them the path, take them on that journey of true knowledge.'

'Or maybe end it all! Maybe not! I can never make up my mind about man. What do you say then is our job, to guide or to judge?'

'We have to be the light within. You judge severely, Krishna. Forgive your mother, she has a woman's heart and a mother's soul. She is greater than Gods, my brother.' The voice of the Buddha then stopped speaking in Krishna's head.

Krishna looked at the unevenly pebbled road ahead of him, and smiled as he breathed in the fumes of the passing cars. The cars honked behind him and he, the God, stepped aside, his back now pressed against the wall of a century-old building, to allow the cars to pass through the narrow gully. The hawker, who stood next to him, spat on the rear of the car. His saliva, orange and frothy from chewing beetle nut, landed on the wall instead.

"Bastards, where do you think the pedestrians should walk?"

Krishna patted the hawker on his shoulder and winked, "We'll be the ones to walk on the clouds, uncle. We are God's chosen ones!"

As he walked further, he spotted ragged beggars sleeping on the kerb. He threw a handful of coins into the air. As the coins flipped in the air, he shouted at the top of his voice, "This is my kind of world."

"Time for a meeting," spoke the now composed Krishna.

SUNDERAMAN'S REWARD

ॐ

In another part of New Delhi, Sunderaman stood studying his appearance in the full-length mirror. "I am handsome, I am young, so how and why can't the young Shiny see me as I was?"

As he looked in the mirror, he noticed a shadow from the corner of his eye as Old Nick appeared beside him. "I can only make you look young in your own eyes, I can't fool everyone."

"You f****r, but you told me so! You said that everyone would see me as the young and handsome man that I once was, you said that Shiny would want me when she saw how handsome I was."

"It was just that I thought that she may have taken to you, I am not always right, you see."

"But you said that you are a God, surely you can make it so?"

"Not always, my friend, but I have given you wealth and riches. You may then tempt her with these gems that I have given you. Surely all the wealth and some charm should get you your girl?"

"And what if she still refuses? What then?"

"Then threaten her."

"How, with what?"

"Blackmail is always effective; use it and the threat of dismissal from her job and for the new doctor that she has taken a shine to."

"Dismiss the new doctor, are you kidding! I am lower down in the hierarchy, he is a full-fledged Master in Surgery and I am not even a Bachelor of Arts. It works like that in our country; you are only as good as your degree," said a forlorn Sunderaman.

Old Nick looked at him for a while before he said, "Look into the mirror, tell me what you see."

Sunderaman did as told and as he looked, he saw nurse Shiny in a lovers' tryst. She was entwined in the arms of the young doctor and they were on the verge of making love.

"What good is this vision to me?" asked Sunderaman.

"Look closer, my friend, where are they?"

Sunderaman looked again. "They are in the store, in the basement, the cheeky little sods, I am not having this. They are in my territory, who let them in?"

"That's right, my friend, go there now and stop them in their tracks. Threaten to tell the Medical Director of what you have seen, and then intimidate the doctor to an extent that he leaves this hospital. After which, when you have the nurse Shiny on her own, give her a pearl or two and then ask her to surrender to you or else!"

"I will, I will do this," shouted the now determined Sunderaman as he ran from his room.

As he ran, Old Nick chuckled as he faded into nothing.

At this very time, Chris appeared in New Delhi; he had made up his mind to hound down Nick although this was his brother's territory. As he walked along the streets and looked at the beggars, he wondered to himself as to what Krishna had been doing.

'All this filth, all this suffering, it is not good!' he thought to himself.

"And where have you come from?" asked the Buddha as he stopped time to talk to the young God. "Is your part of the world any better, is there less filth and suffering in the world that you tend? We are all alike, young Chris. We can only alleviate suffering to an extent, we cannot swap the first world with the third, it's not as simple as that, my brother."

"But look at it, look at the children, look at their amputated limbs! Look at the ones that have lost their sight. They have been dismembered and blinded to arouse sympathy in people, sympathy that can be monetized. It is inhuman, this suffering was not given by us, it is inflicted by man's greed, why allow these monstrous men to live? Why allow this spectacle to continue?"

"Is it any better in the Christian parts of the world, where the old are forsaken and babies abandoned? I think not."

"Well at least I can try to help out here, I can at least find Krishna and help him to send Old Nick on his way, he is not helping the people of this world at all."

"Your spirit is pure, young Chris, however you need to calm down, if you want to help Krishna, then go to him but be aware, other dark forces are treading this world too."

Chris watched as the Buddha faded and then he too faded.

THE BETRAYAL

&

Sunderaman ran down the corridor of the hospital, and as he ran, he bumped into a nurse who was pushing the nursing trolley of one of the patients; the forceps and bottles of medicines were sent flying into the air as he crashed into the trolley.

"Why do you not look where you are going, you useless bitch?" shouted Sunderaman as he ran past her. The nurse cursed him loud and clear. Sunderaman just ploughed on, regardless.

He ran; this coughing and spluttering fat man, he ran as fast as his scarcely used legs could carry him. He had to stop though to catch his breath on the landing of the stairs and as he puffed he thought to himself, 'Thank the Gods that I am going down the stairs rather than up.'

He continued as he had a vested, wicked interest in not letting the new doctor have his wicked way with Nurse Shiny. Eventually he arrived at the basement where the storeroom was situated. He stopped for a second and then regaining his composure, he walked over to the door of the storeroom and putting his ear to the door, he listened to the noises from within.

Loving noises, heavy breathing, kissing noises. He could stand no more and at the end of his tether, he crashed open the door.

"What is going on in here?" shouted Sunderaman at the top of his voice.

The doctor pulled himself away from Nurse Shiny and tried his best to compose himself. Nurse Shiny pulled her clothes back into place.

"We were here for some stocktaking," she said instantly.

"That's right," confirmed the doctor.

"The only stock that you were taking was of each other," shouted Sunderaman. "I saw with my own eyes, you both have had it. Wait till I report this to the Medical Director."

"But we have done nothing wrong!" said the new doctor.

"Nothing wrong, I suggest you button yourself up and get yourself off to the toilet, young man, you are in big trouble. And as for you Nurse Shiny, what do you think that Sister Joana is going to say?"

"Wait, Sunderaman. Mr Sunderaman, perhaps we can come to some arrangement, perhaps we can sort this out amicably." The doctor worked it out quickly in his mind.

"What, you now try to bribe me, not only do you soil one of my storerooms, now you try to soil my character too with your bribes."

"Just a suggestion, we could perhaps work something out, what is it that you really want?" said the young doctor as he looked towards Nurse Shiny.

"You cannot be serious," said the young nurse, "surely you cannot be serious?"

"If it will save our skins, then so be it," replied the young doctor with a sneer.

"You are a bastard, you sick mean dog! What of those entreaties of love; they were no more than pretence? You lied so as to seek my flesh, that's all that you ever wanted? Oh you are sick, you devious dog!"

"We can solve this problem, can we not, great Sunderaman?" asked the young doctor as he ignored Nurse Shiny.

Sunderaman stood and thought for a moment. "I think that I could be persuaded to forget what I have seen if this young, untouched, and lovely little Shiny would favour me now and again."

"Consider it done, great Sunderaman."

"What! You would sell me to him to save your skin?" asked the nurse.

"It will save your skin too, and after all, what is it all about, we are just skin and bones, we must use what we have."

"I won't do it, not on my dead body! And you, who do you think you are, a pimp?"

"Call me a dog, call me a pimp, I don't care. And now you worry about what your parents will say if they find out what has been going on. I have obviously no intention of marrying you, what will become of you and your family's reputation? It's in your best interest that I make a deal with Sunderaman, Nurse Shiny."

Shiny burst into tears as the two men shook hands. She wished for that moment to vanish. The young doctor then went about his business. Sunderaman said to Nurse Shiny, "I will see you in my office in half an hour, make sure that you have washed and that you are wearing clean underwear." He then walked back to his office with a smile on his face.

Old Nick smiled as he had watched all that had happened.

Sometime later, Sunderaman sat in his office and waited. There was a knock on the door.

"Come," said he.

The door opened and in walked nurse Shiny.

"How do you want me?" she asked.

"Oh come now," said Sunderaman. "I am not a monster, here look at this plate of gems on the table, rubies, pearls, even diamonds, help yourself to a few. I will tell you what, I will even lower the lights a little so as you will not have to see so much of me."

"Whatever it is, let's get over and done with it and if you don't hurry I will puke right here."

"Oh come on, I am not so ugly! Now tell me pudding, how should we go about it, will you take off your clothes or do you need some help?" Sunderaman wanted to win her over and hoped that some restraint at this sensitive moment could turn the girl's heart in his favour.

Shiny cringed, standing behind a rack stacked with cartons; she stripped in shame and with revolting disgust for the man who watched her. It was dark where she stood, under the cover of shadow of cartons on the rack, with her head bent; tearful and helpless.

She called out to the God that she knew, the one she had grown up with, The Christ. But the image that came to her mind was not that of Christ in his scarlet robes, but of Krishna, the pantry boy in his blue uniform, grinning and winking.

Sunderaman bent over his table to see her better and drooled with the thought of what was to come. Although he looked on with lust in his mind his penis did not react. His genitals were as flaccid as they were at the start of this game, and he, who had marveled at his capacity for sex, was most disconcerted at his body's refusal to comply with his wishes.

Nurse Shiny was almost naked now but try as he might, the great Sunderaman could not achieve erection.

"What is the matter with you? Why can't you just get over and done with it?" asked nurse Shiny.

"I don't know!" said a perplexed Sunderaman, "what is going on, I am not used to this; it's just that the mind is willing but the flesh seems to be weak."

"Oh, so that was the reason, then, you impotent, fat, mean bastard, all you can do is fantasize about girls. Good, serves you right. And now let me first get into my dress and then we shall talk." Shiny slipped her tunic over her head and stepped back into the skirt. Quickly buttoned and zipped, she walked up to a sheepish Sunderaman, who was jerking himself to attain an erection.

"Don't work too hard, 'its' time is up. And if you want me to keep silent about your impotence then stay quiet about what you know and I will keep my side of the promise. What do you think Sister Joana will say if she learns of your willing mind and weak flesh? You don't want young nurses to mock you, do you?"

With this threat, Shiny walked away and on her way out, she met Krishna.

He grinned at her just the way he had in her mind. Shiny found herself thinking of *Draupadi's* dishonor. The scene from the popular television soap, based on the epic *Mahabharata*, flashed back in her mind as she walked to her room in the Nurses' Hostel.

Draupadi, head bent and palms folded in prayer, *Dushasana* pulling at her robe, and the heap of sari that lay on the floor, as the glorious court of *Kurus* watched their daughter-in-law being stripped in public by her husbands' cousin; the entire episode replayed in Shiny's mind. *Dushasana's* attempt at humiliating *Draupadi* had been foiled by Krishna, who had by his Godly powers turned the sari into an infinite cloth. The more *Dushasana* pulled at it, the longer it became. Thus Krishna saved *Draupadi* the shame of nudity in public.

Shiny bent her head at the altar of the little temple in her room and wept bitterly. Her love had been dashed to smithereens, but her faith stood restored.

Sunderaman looked down on his flaccid penis. 'I am not so old. I still have many years of manhood in me. This is a trick, I am not going to let Nick get away with this!' But in place of Old Nick, Krishna appeared at his side, "How are you doing, sir? Any problems, can I help you with something?" Krishna looked down at Sunderaman's open fly and pointed to the centre-front of his pants.

GODS UNITED

૪૭

Krishna walked away from Sunderaman's office to the store in the basement and as he looked around he noticed that Old Nick was not there.

A moment later, Chris appeared and seeing Krishna before him said, "Brother, at long last we meet again." They looked at each other and then clasped each other within their arms as they tried to catch up with all the missing years.

They both laughed as they talked about the way the world was going and about the adventures that they had experienced recently.

"I saw you on the island after the tsunami, you know, it was just that I did not want to interfere."

"I know brother, I felt your presence, but it was not the right time for us to meet."

"And now?"

"We both know that now is the time, we need to sort out Old Nick, he is going mad and bringing misery but I can't seem to get a hold on where he is now".

"He is still here somewhere. Somewhere he walks this Earth, I can still feel his presence."

"He is here, close, somewhere close, I too can feel him. Come, we will look for him together."

SHINY FINDS HER SELF

❧

Next morning, the young doctor, who had been Shiny's lover till the day before, watched Shiny go past him without a smile or a glance in his direction. He felt slighted and angry that a mere nurse should ignore him. He was miffed that a man with his looks and build should be ignored by a plain Jane. He had expected her to come back to him, with her vulnerable doe-like expression, pleading love. At the very least he would have expected to see a broken, shame-faced woman. But before him was a young woman walking with her head held high, walking with dignity and pride.

'F****** whores! They sleep around with men and then ask their parents to find them a suitable boy! Ugh! So middle class, so Indian!' he said to himself.

"Hey man, I have been hearing these things about you! You know I don't like to interfere in personal matters but I have to maintain the decorum of my ward. What's between you and that doctor?" Sister Joana darted at Shiny as soon as she sighted her in the ward. Shiny felt calm. She managed to retain her composure. Nor did she feel any fear.

"Do you mean that new surgery resident, *Chechi*?"

Joana had expected a nervous squeal and an outright denial of any association with the doctor, but here was a placid counter-question.

"Why, yes my dear! That's what I have been told, by none other than your very best friends, and don't you think you can fool me! And don't give me that ruse about him being your country cousin. He's not even from South India, leave alone your state; so where were we?" Joana put on a stern expression to unnerve Shiny.

"You are right, he's from the North. And yes the girls were not lying about me, I do talk to him, but I am not serious. Much as I may try, I cannot forget what you told us when we were appointed to your ward: 'Never get serious about these doctors because you don't count anywhere in their scheme of things. Focus on your life, they will not think twice before ruining yours.' I remember your speech verbatim, Sister. Just to let you know, I am following your advice on writing NCLEX."

Joana cursed the nursing aides for feeding her with misleading gossip, she should have known better than to trust those idle women. She was not used to nurses proving her wrong. Now she felt impish at having made insinuations without any supporting evidence.

"Ah, NCLEX! But that's a tough exam to clear. Are you thinking of relocating to the US for good? But child, you have a family in Alpe; what about them?" Joana tried to make up for her impropriety by feigning to be Shiny's well-wisher.

"You are not even engaged; would you not rather marry and then relocate to a foreign land? I mean it's not Dubai, it's the US. And the US is vast – it's a world apart from ours. Even the air tickets are prohibitively expensive."

"I am doing this for my family, *Chechi*. Once I have a job, I will be able to sponsor my sister's education here. Also with a salary in dollars we can get any eligible groom in Kerala. You know how grooms can be settled with a neat dowry in our world. Sorry *Chechi*, I must rush. Dr Gupta wants me to assist him with a bedside-dressing. I need to get going now."

'That's an ambitious girl,' thought Joana to herself as she watched her go. 'Maybe she did have a fling with the doctor, maybe he used her, maybe there was nothing, who knows. How I wish I had been smart enough to have bought a groom with dollars. What a waste it was to have hankered after love.' Joana sighed at the thought of love. 'It still hurts, it doesn't improve with time.'

A FLOWER

౮ఄ

Nick saw his plans ruined as Sister Shiny walked away from his trap. He thought it best to abandon a distraught and angry Sunderaman, who had been rendered impotent by Krishna. 'This Krishna is a wily guy,' he thought to himself. He worked out a plan in his mind unaware that Chris was in the city to seek him out.

"Did you take it up with Krishna again, mother? Wait, can I call you *Ma*, like Krishna does. It's a small thing that I ask of you; surely Krishna will not object to that? I have accepted his verdict on everything, mother, have I not?" Nick cast a sly glance at Krishna's icon in the temple.

"I have little influence over Krishna, my child. He does not wish you to stay with us, and I can't force him. If I push him too much, he will go away. He has this quirk of vanishing for months and then reappearing when he has reconciled with those who have wronged him. You don't understand because you have not had to put up with humiliation, you had a regular childhood, and my Krishna, he has led a hard life; being a bastard is not easy. Forgive me son, I can only meet you in his absence. Should I get you something to eat? I made some rice and lentils this morning."

Yashoda got about serving lunch; she was spring in her step. Her eyes were wet with kindness and memories of yesteryears. She thought of her ex-lover in a mellow light, she recalled the tender moments of togetherness. All the love that she had felt for him some 20 years ago returned in that moment. Nick was a child her lover had borne with his wife, but he felt like her own.

147

Nick had been plotting to use Yashoda against her own son, but his plans hit a stumbling block every now and then. He had little hope of harming Krishna by regular means of poisoning or physical harm. He would have to come up with a plan that would be invincible and foolproof. He looked at Yashoda and wondered if he should take her away, from Krishna, to his own land of sin? How would Krishna react? Could Krishna be forced to meet him on his turf? Nick thought of all the wicked plans that he could conjecture; apprehensive on the one hand and cautious on the other. He knew that a slip at this point would be cataclysmic.

"Here child, I saved some *prasad* for you, have some till I warm the lentils for you." Yashoda dished out some rice pudding in a saucer and held it out to Nick.

'It is all getting too mushy with mother-son emotions, to hell with her. I cannot keep playing this act for too long,' Nick thought to himself, smiling all along as he accepted the pudding. Yashoda drew the curtain in her temple and thanked Krishna, her lord, for bringing her other son into her life. Krishna's icon was now in full view and the sight of Krishna with a flute threw Nick into a bout of rage. He flung the bowl high. 'Why is it that these human beings, who are at my mercy, worship other Gods? Why can't they be a slave to me, the God of misfortune?'

"So you want to thank your God for me? Why, because I am your lover's son, isn't that so?" Nick walked up to the temple and drew the curtain back. Yashoda was amazed at the sudden change that had come over Nick.

"You remain a slave to your love, you woman! You do not have the grace and equanimity which is becoming of a mother!"

Nick continued with the accusations, not allowing Yashoda to explain herself or gainsay him. "You do not deserve human life. Why do you pray so hard when you have been given a body to toil and a mind to think? Since you like it so much here, then let us give you an excuse to live here at your God's feet. You have spent years praying to your God but your *vasnas* hold on to you. Therefore, I, Nick, the God of Evil, now turn you into a flower."

In that moment Yashoda turned into a marigold; yellow and bright but chillingly still and silent. She lay on the floor waiting to be picked up by her son. She lay quietly, ashamed that she had not heeded her son, sad that her life had come to an abrupt end, and repentant for trusting an impostor. She had been deceived yet again.

As Nick walked out of the *chawl,* he ran into a furious Sunderaman.

"Hey, you stop! Just where do you think you are going? You promised me a woman and now you have turned me into a no-man, worse than before. I cannot even savour my own wife now, you have ruined me! I should have known better than to have placed my trust in an Evil God, but I will not allow you to leave till you return my manhood," Sunderaman caught at his collar and pulled his face within inches of his own, breathing down hard with anger. Nick felt Sunderaman's foul breath on his face as he pulled away and said, "Take your hands off me. I told you not to mess with me, now leave my shirt alone! I say take your hands off me." As Nick screamed, Sunderaman tightened his hold around his neck.

"Don't you try to scare me, you know nothing, not even proper magic. The local magicians do better tricks than you, you filthy conman! Now listen to me, reverse this whole thing, give me my virility back," Sunderaman shook Nick, who stood firm on his ground.

Nick feared Krishna's wrath. Any minute now Krishna would come to seek him out.

He was only a smaller God. He had to reach his domain, his private heaven before Krishna reached him. But for this imp of a man he would have been home by now. He stopped in his steps and glowered at Sunderaman, who was not to be daunted by rebukes and threats.

"For the last time, Sunderaman, go away! Every minute that you intercept me takes me closer to my end, and I have business to finish.

I cannot die, not yet. So go back to the jewels that I have given you, and live happily with your family!" Nick disengaged himself from Sunderaman's hold.

"Go away! Do you think I can go away to where I came from! Not till you have reversed your magic. Take your money and gems with you, I don't need them. Just return to me my manhood, my ability to perform! I refuse to be an impotent man, even a dog's life is better than this!" Sunderaman was moved to tears every time he mentioned his loss. He had been weeping for two days now, jerking himself in the toilet with tears streaming down his cheeks. He was ashamed to face Shiny or any woman.

"Is that what you think, Mr. Sunderaman? Do you really believe a dog's life is good? Then have it your way!" Nick cast his evil glance once more. Before Sunderaman could take his words back, he had been turned into a pathetic mongrel. Nick laughed at the sight of what stood before him: a dirty, fat mongrel barking relentlessly.

"Oh come on, you can have as much sex as you like now. You are a very virile, healthy dog now, Sunderaman. Bye and say hello to Krishna if you meet him." Nick vanished.

A little later, passersby saw an agitated strange dog. They shooed him away but he was not to be rebuffed.

"Is this a dog or an angry young man? You cannot scare him away. He barks as if he is challenging us all to a duel," a jobless, young man joked to another man who seemed idle and bored. These unemployed young men were always looking for excitement on the roads to pass their time.

"Maybe we should inform the municipality department to have him picked up and eventually put to sleep," they suggested.

Some young urchins, who had been playing cricket on the kerb, now joined the fun. They threw stones at the barking dog. The dog barked harder.

Adjusting to a new life takes time.

JAYWICK

ॐ

Krishna stood in his room in the *chawl*, with his friend Chris, beholding the flower that lay on the table. It was a yellow marigold with a tinge of sadness. He lifted it to his eyes and wept.

"We should have anticipated it, Chris. We are no Gods, we are as helpless as men, my brother!" Krishna thought of his mother's face and how she had suffered for having loved people without discernment.

"I promise you Nick's end, my brother! Can't we undo his magic?" Chris ran the tips of his fingers over the soft petals.

"She is dead, my brother, and she will not even have a pyre! I lament her end. Did she not deserve last rites? But here she is reduced to a flower. I will take this flower to the banks of the Ganges and offer her to the Holy River. After which I will shave my head and take a vow to kill that impostor."

"If that is what you must do, then you must do it," said Chris and then tearfully added, "Farewell then, my brother, but let me go after Nick myself. You must grieve now, what you have lost. Flower she may be but she has a soul. Let's pray for her soul." Chris faded and made himself into nothing.

******

Heavenly Jaywick. East Coast of England. This was Old Nick's land, his version of Heaven in his eyes, Hell maybe in the eyes of others. Here, although it was only a short distance along the coast from

151

Clacton-on-Sea, it was always quite cold. Here he could step out of his version of Jaywick and straight into the real Jaywick, in the wink of an eye, but he seldom visited the real coastal town as it bored him immensely.

Here in his version of Jaywick, the sea was always calm and quite characterless. There was no wind and always a slight drizzle in the air. No birds flew here, it was gull free and always quiet. As quiet as the grave. When souls had passed over and came here, there was no welcoming committee, unlike the heavenly version of Clacton. Old Nick liked to let the new arrivals fend for themselves, survival of the fittest was the order of the day here.

The only thing to relieve the monotony was the occasional flash of lightning, otherwise Jaywick was quite quiet and extremely dull; it was the real Hell.

Nick was soaking in a warm bath; his eyes shut to soak in the sensuous pleasure – hedonism was the theory he had propagated to mankind. He smiled at his victory; modern man lived for pleasure, pleasure was man's constant pursuit. He thought to himself, with satisfaction – if I can convert all men to my way of thinking, they will kill each other for gratification of their personal desires. He smiled to himself. The water felt hot and titillating, all his worries melted in that sensation.

His mates, a two-headed lizard and a three-headed dog, caressed his feet. They were playful, reverential and servile towards their master, their God in Jaywick. They had made up a bath game amongst themselves – rubbing in the lather, licking it off the master, and then soaping him all over again; the game was in doing it faster than the other. Nick enjoyed watching his bath mates vie with each other for his admiration.

Two naked eunuchs with sagging breasts arrived with a tub of rose water mixed in saffron milk. They bathed Nick and his mates with a tender touch. Soon they were joined by men and women whose genitals had been severed and whose faces were distorted. It was their turn to bathe their master and his playmates with blood. Nick was pleased with himself that day. On such days he would invite his followers to an orgy in his chamber.

After he had been bathed by his select, ardent followers, Nick slipped into his silk bathrobe, humming to himself a song he had composed in the bath.

'I must be on a high to be composing music every day,' he thought to himself.

They were waiting for him to arrive; the beasts and the eunuchs, the men and the women, the reptiles and the quadrupeds – all slaves to their only master. Nick's chamber was a haven of evil, the beds were adorned with gems, satin sheets were spread out, and silk curtains veiled the bed. In the chamber were the most hideous looking creatures, neither human nor animals, waiting upon their master. The band in the hall, adjacent to the chamber, played hard rock music.

Nick chose an Elvis Presley costume from his wardrobe. The hideous creatures dressed their master and the eunuchs made up his face.

"Now listen, all of you, my friends, my devoted followers, I love you all! Will you, for the sake of my happiness, rejoice with me tonight?" Nick screamed into the microphone. He stood on his bed and waved his hands, jumping with delight at his own words, and his followers howled in joy. They squealed and obeyed, possessed by their master's voice.

"Raise your hands up and say, we love you."

"We love you!" They beat their chests and wept with joy. It was a delirious moment for the master and his slaves. From his bed he jumped down to the floor and went to each of his followers, raising their hands to his lips, kissing someone's forehead, and embracing another.

Once they were all done, he joined the band in the hall. Wall-to-wall screens were mounted behind the band, and as the lights went down in the room, the screens came alive. Behind Nick was his image, larger than him. On the television screen, behind him, his face radiated with the joy of victory.

"This is our moment of victory. We have beaten the human race and it is the beginning of their end. They will either join us here to live the way we do or be doomed forever. They have lost faith and you have found yours. Here I stand in your midst, lover to you all, a friend to you! There are no rules here that you may not break, passions run unbridled, all sins may be committed without remorse, and nothing is forbidden here. No longer are we men or women, we are neither animal nor human, the line between genders and species blurs here, and you are all my children. Soon you will produce your own children with single-cell reproduction! Wait till my team of scientists accomplishes auto re-generation of cells. This is our moment to celebrate, let the celebrations begin." Nick turned to face the instrumentalists and signalled them to start.

The band started to play an original score that Nick had composed in his moment of reverie, smoke bellowed from the smoke-machines, and marijuana cigarettes were passed around. The mob broke into mad applause and sang with the band. Nick jumped on his followers, they lifted him on their raised hands, and some tried to embrace him. In this barbaric celebration, what with pushing and jostling, some creatures were choked and hurt – but nothing stopped. Such was the rule that governed in Jaywick: each to his own.

Music tore through the hall and those who wanted to dance moved forward, the smokers fell into the side rows, and those who felt horny indulged in sex play. Some simulated oral sex with toys, others splashed their ejaculate on the walls – they played all the time in Jaywick. Nothing was to be revered here.

Nick sang with the main vocalist and laughed at his creation. 'Oh! How pleasing are my principles of aesthetics, how lovely are my creations, and how absurd is my philosophy!' The party faded slowly and all the creatures crawled to their territories, bodies spent out and minds lulled into sleep. They could neither think nor worry. Reflection and meditation were never mentioned in this land, this alternative Jaywick. Sensual pleasure reigned supreme here.

A DOG'S LIFE

∞

In the city of New Delhi, as the day dawned, the dust rose from the roads to fill the air. But as soon as it settled down again and the thick, grey mist of suspended particles from the vehicles dispersed, a dog caught the attention. He seemed to be *enjoying* with his counterpart. It grunted and growled once he had finished the act and sighed with pleasure. The bitch, now standing aloof, stared at the dog.

"Why do you stare, bitch, you have had your fun, now be off," growled the dog.

She was quite a good-looking bitch, the dog thought.

But the dog that Sunderaman had become could take no more of the staring and so barked fiercely at the bitch till she ran away. He stood still for a moment and then, realizing that he had satisfied one of his hungers, went in search of food. He found a vomit as he ran through the streets and ate it mindlessly. But he was still hungry and, thus, carried on with his food hunt. He eventually came to an open gutter and as he stuck his snout into the filthy water he saw his reflection. It was right there; staring back at him was the face of Sunderaman. It was at this moment that the man/dog's brain engaged with reality and he realized what had happened to him. He felt physically sick and started to heave up his guts at the thought of what he had been doing.

'Have I really coupled with a dog? Have I really been eating the bile? What has become of me?' In despair, the dog then took off into the city. Walking for miles, he looked around, saw things that he really could not understand. Small children were begging on the streets. He saw young girls, who had put themselves up for sale; the homeless, who slept on the pavements and had to scavenge heaps of rubbish for food. The rich threw away their half-eaten meals and the poorest of the poor lived off it. It was abominable and piteous that while one man feasts, his fellow human being waits for him to discard the food he did not want. The dog grew pensive.

'People should not have to live like this. I would not treat even a dog the way these people are being treated, well at least not while I am one.' The dog walked some more while wondering, 'What am I thinking? When I was a human, I treated all human beings as if they were animals. Oh, how wrong I was!'

After a bit of more walking and thinking, the dog decided that he would go back to his office at the hospital; after all, it was still his office, whether he was a dog or a man. He arrived at the hospital some time later.

"Hey you, dog, where do you think you are going?" asked a security guard.

"I am going to my office you f****r," replied the dog.

"F*****g bark at me, will you," shouted the security guard as he ran towards the dog with his stick out, ready to beat him into submission.

The dog stood his ground, at this time he still hadn't fully realized his predicament. As the security guard ran towards him with the stick raised, he barked even more.

"Who do you think you are?" barked the dog, "Do you not know who I am, can you not see, it is I, Sunderaman".

The security guard listened as the dog barked and then losing his temper, he hit it as hard as he could with his stick.

"F***! I really am a dog." With these barks, he ran back into the slums of New Delhi.

"F*****g dog, I showed him who the boss was," said the smug security guard to himself as he carried on with his business.

In the city, the dog that Sunderaman had become now walked sadly through the streets alone. He had realized what he had become and all that he had been doing. He had leered at women in his human life. He and his friends had believed that as the way things were for the real men, to use and discard women. For men such as him, wives and daughters were to be strictly guarded and kept indoors, while the other women were meant merely for consumption. He had fantasized about women, undressed them in his mind, and treated them like objects to rev up his libido. Now, as a dog, when he saw people in poor states and was saddened by their predicaments, he wondered how reprehensible and selfish he had been in the human form, treating all and sundry as worthless chattel.

Sunderaman continued to live out the dog's life. The bitch that he had coupled with earlier made advances to him. But now he had no desire to mate with her again. Seeing that she was hungry, he showed her where they could forage for food. The two dogs became friends and it was not long before Sunderaman realized that she was pregnant.

One day when these two dogs were in the slums foraging for food they saw a young boy playing in the street. The dog didn't pay much attention till he heard the loud roar of a motorcycle engine approaching. Being a dog, his hackles were soon up as he stood ready to protect himself. It was then that he saw that the young child had run into the street and was about to be run over by a motorcycle. He ran towards the young child and pushed him off the road as the motorcyclist raced away. At the same time, a man came out from a doorway and seeing the dog knocking over the small boy, went at him with a stick.

"Why are you beating that dog?" asked an old woman, who was a witness to the incident.

"That dog had attacked my son," came the reply.

"You fool, you are like the many other men, always ready to use a stick before you know the truth; that dog never attacked your son, but saved his life". She then went on to explain what had happened.

The man, after having heard the story, bent down to pat the dog, "I am truly sorry, dog," he said. His son then came to his father and looking at the dog, he too started to pat it. "Can we keep him, *baba*?" asked the boy, "I have always wanted a dog."

"I am sorry, my dearest one, but we struggle to fill our own bellies, how can we feed this one too?" The father scratched at his white stubble and the crow-feet around his eyes drew into deep lines as he frowned at the prospect of providing for another being.

"But *baba*, he saved my life," urged the boy.

"But how will we feed him?"

"Please let's keep him," said the boy "I will try a little harder to collect money. Look, he likes you too." The dog wagged his tail.

"Give me another one; all that this dog wants is free food. Well let's see if we can find him an old bone to chew on," said the father as he walked off to the back of their house.

"He is a good man, my *baba*," said the beggar boy to the dog, "He will let you stay, but you will have to behave." The dog wagged his tail again and then licked the boy's face. Together the two played as they pretended to fight. The father was touched to see his son happy and laughing. He watched them play for a while and when the two of them calmed down, he threw a bone at the dog. The Sunderaman part was quite disgusted at the bone but the dog part went into the dog-mode and chewed on the bone, deliriously happy.

"Well he is a happy dog, I will give you that," said the father. "Have you thought of a name for him?"

"Not yet *baba*, I will call him,,, hm... perhaps, we can decide together, dog, come here," shouted the boy.

"Well," said the father, "what is your name to be?" he asked of the dog.

The dog looked at the two humans and as he looked he pawed an "S" in the sand before them.

"Look father he has drawn the letter "S", perhaps his name is Sunny."

"Sunny, he is too ugly to be called Sunny, Shitface, more like it! Don't frown, I was joking. You can call him as you please but remember, you have to try to get enough money and food so that we can feed him. Don't take him along when you go begging, you may scare or repulse a few patrons."

"I will get all he needs father. I will tie him to a pole, when I go. *Ammi* need not keep an eye on him then, and that way Sunny won't be a bother at all," replied the boy as he ran off to play with the dog.

So it was then that the dog became a part of this poor family. He was loved and fed as well as these poor people could manage. But it was not long before the pregnant bitch returned in Sunderaman's life.

It was early one morning when she arrived. She looked half-starved although her belly was by now quite bloated with the ever growing puppies that were inside her. The dog looked at her and if a dog could cry, he would have done so. He led her to where his fresh water was and gave her what scraps of food he had, but he noticed that it was not enough. Thereafter, he went to find his new master.

"What is it Sunny?" asked the boy as the dog rubbed his nose on the now waking boy. "What's up doggy?"

Sunderaman pulled at the boy with his teeth and eventually the young fellow understood that he should follow the dog.

He followed Sunderaman into the common courtyard.

"What's wrong with her?" asked the boy upon seeing the bitch. The bitch lay on the ground, heaving and exhausted. The boy stroked the bitch, "Hey, she is all bones, she needs feeding Sunny," he said and ran off to the kitchen to look for food. A few minutes later, he returned with the whole family's rations and fed it to the female dog.

A little later there was a scream from the kitchen. "We have been robbed," screamed the boy's mother, "All our food has gone!"

The boy's father was awakened by the scream and he too came running down into the kitchen. "Look!" shouted the mother, "All the rice and curry has vanished! It's that evil child of Najma, he steals from everybody's house in the neighbourhood, the demon that he is!"

"Shut up you dumb woman! Don't you make allegations without first finding the truth; we have enough troubles to tide us over. It is only one meal, but if Salim hears your accusations against his son, he will not spare me. We can always find enough money to get more rations. We will get by till tomorrow, somehow. Don't fret now."

"But where has our food gone?" she screamed.

The boy's father looked out into the yard and saw the bloated dog lying in the sand with Sunny and the boy, "I think I can guess," he said.

The father walked out into the yard and asked his son, "What have you been up to, you mischievous boy?"

"It is Sunny's friend father, she was hungry, look I think that she is unwell, for all you know she is dying!"

"So, you gave her our food, you fed her two people's meal! Did you?" asked the father.

"She was hungry father!" said the young boy in reply.

"Your *Ammi* is hungry, I am hungry, would you feed the animals before we can feed ourselves?"

The boy stared at his father and after thinking for a while he burst into tears.

"We will not starve today, my little saint, we have a little money left and we can afford some scraps of food but we cannot afford another dog. Especially a pregnant one. The bitch is not sick, she is expecting a litter. When the puppies are born, not only will they break us apart financially but they will also break our hearts. We will feed her today and that is it, then she will have to go. No child, I won't have any more of this dog nonsense!"

As this conversation progressed, the dog sat, watched, and listened. He also watched as the boy took the money from his father and went off to the shop at the end of the road to buy some food.

'This is not right,' thought the dog, 'These are good people and they deserve better.' With these thoughts in his head, he walked out of the yard and made his way back to the hospital where he had worked as a human. The dog had the makings of a plan, formulating in his head.

Sunderaman had now taken over the control of the dog's mind and he was now thinking with the skill and cunning of his old human self. He was at this moment thinking of the gems and gold hidden in the chest in his office.

The dog stealthily approached the hospital. He was wiser from his last visit to the hospital that he could not just walk in. So he sat, watched, and waited.

At about 1 in the morning an ambulance came speeding up to the entrance. The dog watched all the security personnel run about to fetch a stretcher and one of the security guards placed a call to the nurse in-charge to wheel the patient to the Emergency Triage. Slyly, the dog took cover under a mobile stretcher that had been brought out from inside the hospital to fetch the patient. The dog used every skill he knew as a man to make his way to his old office, and he also took the opportunity to use the skill of the dog that he had become to look out for any traps that might be placed in his way. He walked down the corridors and on hearing any noise, he hid till it was safe again to proceed on his way.

Eventually, he found himself in front of the door to his old office and jumping up, he pushed down on the door handle to open it. As he entered his old office, he saw the chest below his old table, just where he had left it. He then proceeded as best he could to open the chest, biting and clawing at the latch. It was strange how the gems had lost their sparkle to his doggy eyes, but he knew from his instinct that they were worth a lot of money.

He looked around the office and eventually his eyes fell upon a jute bag that he used to carry his big tiffin box in. 'That will do nicely,' said he as he took it over to the chest and began to nose and mouth in as many gems and as much gold as he could. It did not take long to fill but then the hard thing was to work the bag over his head so that he could carry it.

Then, stealthily, the dog worked his way out of the hospital.

"Oye, you, dog," came a familiar voice, "What have I told you about coming around here begging? Be off!" shouted the security guard as he looked around for stones to throw at him. The dog did not need the telling twice. He was off and running at a speed, wanting to get back to his new home, back to the people and dogs that loved him.

It was dawn when he reached home. He saw that the boy, and the female dog, were sleeping still in the yard. He walked over to the boy and after working the bag off of his shoulders he laid it at the boy's feet.

"Hello Sunny!" said the boy as he yawned himself awake.

The dog growled softly and then grabbed the boy's arm gently in his mouth as he guided him to the bag that he had set out before him.

"What is this?" asked the boy of the dog. He yelled on seeing the precious contents of the bag, "What! What is this Sunny? Where did you find it? I had better go and show it to *baba*. You didn't steal it, did you?"

The boy ran off and after some time he returned with his smiling father. The man looked at the dog and then asked it, "But where did you find these gems, Sunny?"

The dog just sat on the sand and wagged his tail happily, he then walked over to the female and sat next to her so as the man knew that he wanted her to be looked after as well.

"Yes, I know that hero, I know that you want your girl to be taken care of. With what you have brought us, we can afford to look after both of you. But where did you find these gemstones? Are they stolen?"

He just jumped and ran in circles as he chased his tail.

"Well he seems happy enough, son," said the man.

"Will you hand them to the police?" asked the boy.

The man looked at his son and laughed, "Sometimes I forget just how old you are, my dearest little saint; you have a lot to learn. No we will not hand them to the police. They would just steal them and spend them on themselves. No, this is our windfall and it will feed us and your animals for some time to come."

A QUESTION OF FAITH

৪৩

In another part of the planet, just out of sync from the real world, Chris appeared on the shore of the coastline that was his new heaven. This was his version of Clacton-on-Sea and he loved it here. He looked at the calm sea that ebbed and flowed before him; it had character, this coastline, and it always made him smile. Today, there was no wind and the air was quite peaceful. A slight drizzle filled the air and he smiled again as he felt the soft drops of rain brushing his face. Chris's smile broadened as he realized that there were no birds, for they had migrated to continue with their lives. 'Well,' he thought, 'this too adds to the peace and complexity of it all. So, peaceful, as quiet as the grave perhaps. Even a grave has its beauty, otherwise why would we make them and then continue to tidy them? This really is heaven.'

He then stood and looked over to the next village. He could just see the skyline over Jaywick from where he stood. It seemed funny how the skyline could change so dramatically; he even thought that he could see the crackling of thunderbolts in the sky. 'Perhaps it is just my imagination,' he thought.

'Oh well, time I was on my way to sort things out with Old Nick.' Then he faded.

Chris reappeared on a hilly knoll overlooking the river Mekong in a faraway land. 'This is not how it usually happens,' he thought to himself. 'I usually end up where I want to go.' He stood and studied the landscape and then as he turned he saw floating about two feet from the ground the Buddha himself – Buddy Roy.

"Hello Roy, I might have guessed."

"It is time that we had a chat, my boy," spake the Buddha.

"I have to go to him, you know I do. He has created such discontent. He is so evil. Why did he have to go and kill Krishna's mother? Does he not realize what a temper Krishna has, does he not know how upset Krishna is, how upset I am, and there will be repercussions you know? He has unbalanced the world with his meddling. He must pay, you know, he really must. I must sort this out before Krishna reaches the banks of the Ganges."

"Be calm, young Chris," replied the Buddha in a calming tone. "All will be well, take some deep breaths and calm yourself. Her time had come anyway, Chris. She is not a God, she had to die sometime. Now don't you get yourself into a flurry and go about behaving like Nick."

"But you have seen what he has done, how can I be calm? I must go to his heaven, the Hell that it is, and sort this out."

"And what will you do? Will you smite him with fireballs? Will you cause the Earth to quake? A plague of locusts, perhaps?"

"Locusts will do no good; he does not really live so how will they help?"

"Aha," smiled the Buddha.

Chris stood and thought for a moment. "I see what you mean, I can't kill him, can I?"

"No, you cannot."

"And Krishna?"

"No, neither you nor Krishna. Not even myself, or any of the other Gods for that matter can actually kill him. We do not have that sort of power; all we can do is discredit him and hope that the mortals will cease to believe in him, only then will he truly cease to be."

"But he has done so many wrongs, he has hurt so many people, he has killed Krishna's mother and even turned one man into a dog."

"The man who is a dog now, he will learn from his experience. Perhaps it will make him a better person when he is returned to human form, who knows. As for Yashoda, she has moved on into another sphere of existence, that's all. And now my young friend, you must rest and in meditation work out the next part of this mysterious jigsaw puzzle."

"But he is evil, something must be done about him," said Chris.

"He is only a small part of this ongoing existence that we all endure, he plays his part and he plays it well, you too must play your part and play it as well as he does."

Chris stood for a moment as he thought of what the Buddha had told him. He looked quite perplexed by it all.

"He will always be believed in, every living person will always believe in some sort of evil, we cannot discredit him enough for the human race not to believe in him."

"All the sentient beings must be able to believe in everything. Come and sit by me Chris, we will meditate together."

As the Buddha and Chris floated next to each other, calm descended all over the world. After a while when all was quite quiet, the Buddha faded and left Chris to meditate on his own for a while.

In distant India, Krishna picked up a razor. He looked at the blade as it rested in his hand and smiled at his reflection.

JAYWICK, KINGDOM OF HELL

&

O ld Nick sat on a cloud and looked down on the Earth below. He had tired quite quickly of all the noise. He hated the loud noises really but he was not about to tell anyone. He also hated all the toadies that followed after him, these sycophants that agreed with his every word. What he would give for just one of them to have a decent argument with him, but no.

He had been cursed to look after the dead souls of the ones that wanted everything. These greedy little beings that would creep up to him and agree to everything that he demanded. It quite astonished him at times as to how far these souls would go just to be assured that they would have all that they wanted. He had disfigured quite a lot of them and they still believed in his virtue. He had taken from them all that they had loved and still they worshipped him in the hope that they would one day have all that they craved for.

Old Nick wound up the party that he had thrown shortly after it had started; he had grown weary of it very quickly and had sent all his worshippers off with a headache. 'That will teach the toadying bastards,' he thought. Now he sat on a cloud as he looked down towards the Earth and the land of the living. 'What joys are these humans even now having, what joys and what heartaches? At least these beings have a diverse life, they have no knowing of what is to become of them. They can enjoy their quick little existences and all I can do is watch. They can experience love and death and all I can do is watch. Is it any wonder that I get frustrated and with this frustration comes my anger? Is it no wonder that I want to interfere with their lives, as I have nothing to do but to watch as they live them? To watch in wonder and jealousy. Why do they not know how lucky they are?'

Nick smiled as he drew from his pocket a deck of cards and then pointed his finger at a bank in the heart of London as he threw the card towards it, and on that day the shares in this bank collapsed, sending ripples around the world. Nick threw a few more cards Earthwards and people suffered as their investments collapsed and as confidence was lost in commerce, more and more people suffered. He pointed his finger at America and threw another card and the winds and snows of winter took hold, more and more people suffered because of this. He then cast his gaze over to Africa, this was always one of his favourite places and as he looked down he drew out the ace of spades and threw it downwards. The waters evaporated to cause the worst drought that this country had seen yet, and more and more humans suffered.

"Oh it is this easy when you are a God," said Old Nick to himself as he settled down on his cloud. But he was now getting tired and bored, even with all this chaos. "If only I had a friend, someone to share all this with, perhaps then I would be happy?"

In Delhi, Krishna smiled as he looked at the reflection in the razor blade, for there smiling back at him was his own face. This heavenly face had a way of calming down all humans that looked at it so why should it not have the same effect on a God? He knew he was expected to remain calm and he had the calm coming into him in spasms. It raged, this calm. Just a moment ago he had felt as if he could smash the world to bits, but now he felt different and then in another moment he would be angry all over again.

Krishna stared at the blade that he held in his hand and thought of Old Nick, 'Oh that I could caress his neck with this blade.'

Krishna smiled at his reflection in the blade and thought of the Ganges. He knew that Buddha would reason with him and Chris would send him peace messages on Facebook and through the spirit world. Krishna allowed himself to think for a moment longer, after which he decided to look for his answers in the Ganges.

In Heavenly Clacton-on-Sea, Chris had found his answer. He had enjoyed his meditation but it was now time to return to his own Heaven and prepare for the assault on Krishna. This assault was not a warlike thing but more of a way to stop his brother from making war on his enemies. He was calm now and his thoughts seemed clearer. Chris would intercept his brother as soon as possible and try to talk some sense into him. Little did he know of what was about to happen.

Haridwar. Resonating gongs and the public address system of the Vishnu temple, built at the most sacred spot of *Har Ki Pauri* on the banks of the River Ganges, announced evening *aarti*. At dusk, *Har Ki Pauri*, the most visited and revered *ghat* in Haridwar, becomes the locus of action in the city. It was beginning to get dark and thousands of pilgrims stopped all personal activity to watch the grand spectacle of a ritual that the *ghat* witnessed at twilight every day. Flames in the fire bowls rose with the gush of incoming breeze from the sacred river. The priests, who had descended to the edge of the *ghat*, waited for their signal to start *Ganga aarti*.

Some visitors had come by for a pilgrimage and others for a bath and cleansing after immersing the ashes of the dead in the Ganges.

Ashes were immersed in the waters of another *ghat*, close by.

Two days after the cremation, the ashes are collected and brought to Haridwar for immersion. No matter where you live, a Hindu has to travel all the way to Haridwar for the last rites. After immersing the last remains, the members of the bereaved family proceed to *Har Ki Pauri* for a holy dip. Even on this day many men stood on the most sacred banks of the Ganga, bidding their last farewell to their loved ones.

All the devotees, who had come to participate in the prayer, prepared to light the wick in their earthen *diyas*. Once the *diya* had been lit, they carefully placed it along with flowers on a leaf that they would set afloat in the Ganges at the culmination of *aarti*. Soon after the prayer ritual, inky waters of the river came to be illumined with hundreds of *diya* boats. Many visitors stayed back after the temple ritual of the evening *aarti* to watch these lit boats become twinkling little dots in the distance. The sight of twinkling boats merge into dark nothingness, calmed even the most turbulent of souls. The lamp boats were hopes that men sent out to the Goddess Ganga – 'Eventually, all wishes are meant to fade away. No one is given all,' Ganga said to the dainty, little, sparkling boats.

Earthen *diya*, leaf, flowers, and wick were all sold together as one pack by flower-sellers who did brisk business on the banks of the *ghat*. The wide concrete pavement that led to the steps of the *ghat* served as a busy flea market and beggars' spot. Here the hawkers found easy customers in pilgrims and beggars didn't have to try too hard to coax pilgrims to part with their money.

Within minutes of the announcement of *aarti,* the atmosphere was charged with prayers and resounding gongs. Priests moved the fire bowl in circles, raising it to the skies and lowering it to touch the cold waters. Hymns in praise of the Ganges filled the banks. The sounds of gongs and prayers along with the sight of flames moving in circles caused a trance-like effect on the minds of the spectators.

Krishna drowned his grief in the waters of the Ganga.

The river was more than a water body; it was a living character from ancient myths. It was a mother, wife, and daughter – the feminine, benevolent provider. He stood a long time, caught in an eddy of tears that men and women had wept in the river. He stood at the *Gau Ghat,* where men immersed the ashes of the dead. He felt drenched in the pain of mankind. In the distance he could see the flickering light boats ride the waves of the river. The boats of hope and prayer sent to him, the God of Gods.

His rage had subsided and the thought to avenge his mother's death had passed into nothingness. He was calm and still, like the ripples of the caressing Ganga. He took one more dip and chanted the celestial hymn known only to the Gods.

In Sunderaman's office, the Buddha floated. He was about a foot off the floor and as he floated, he thought good thoughts. In front of him was a computer screen on the table. 'These are such wonderfully modern things,' he thought, 'surely we can do some good with them.'

The Buddha, who floated so serenely with his hands on his legs, suddenly raised his arms and gave a gentle push to the nothingness before him.

Close to the office the dog, that Sunderaman had become, woke from his slumber and noticed straightaway that something was wrong; his friend, the boy sweated profusely and was delirious with fever as his father attended to him. The dog edged cautiously towards the man as he cradled his son in his arms.

"Oh you wonder what is wrong, do you? You saved my boy's life once, I know, but now somehow he has caught a chill and he may die from it. Life is funny, isn't it, you save my boy, we take you in and then my boy once again leans towards his death. Is death chasing him?"

The dog looked at what was happening and then ran from the yard where the family was. He ran and ran and ran. He knew where he was heading. After his long run he found himself at the hospital where he had worked as a human being, here he knew that he could get the help and the wealth that he needed. He stood and panted, waited until the security guard had turned his back and then ran into the hospital to his office.

"*Oye* you," came the cry from the security guard as he saw Sunderaman, the dog, run past. The security guard chased but he was not fast enough. Then just as he was about to go back, he saw the dog once again.

"I have you now," he shouted. "This is a dead end," and as he chased, he saw the dog stop before Sunderaman's office, push down the door lever and enter the office. "I have you now dog," he said with a smile as he now slowed his pace to get back his breath.

As the dog entered his old office, he was surprised to see a man floating in front of the computer screen.

"Surprised are you, Sunderaman?" asked the Buddha.

The dog barked but actually spoke the words, "Well, yes."

"And so you should be, it is not every day that a human meets a God."

"You know that I am a human then?" Sunderaman asked as he then cowered before the Buddha and shook in fear as he carried on, "But why do I keep meeting Gods?"

"Stand up and be a man Sunderaman, do not cower before me like a dog, I am here to help you."

"You want me to stand on all four legs, do you?"

"Stand up and look into the mirror; you are no longer a dog. You are back to what you once were although I suspect that now you are a better person for all the things that have happened to you. Why else have you come here?"

Sunderaman stood tall, as he had done before as a human, and he then looked into the office mirror and there in the reflection he saw himself as a human.

"I am back to my old self," he said as he turned towards the Buddha. But the Buddha was no longer there.

It was at this time that the door crashed open and the security guard came running in. "Sunderaman!" said he in surprise. "I am surprised to see you but where is the dog?"

"Dog, what dog?"

"The dog that just came running into this office, where is it?"

"I have seen no dog here, only you," replied the now smiling Sunderaman.

"I am surprised at you, have you started keeping pets in your office, I saw a dog run in here and I want to know where it is! But wait, I thought you were missing yourself."

"Missing? Oh yes, I was on a break from mankind."

"Are you kidding me Sunderaman, you resurface after months, then let a dog into your office, and now you give me fluffy explanations. I know what you are all about, you greedy pig! Don't even try to mess with me. "

"Go find the dog then," Sunderaman stepped aside.

He really did not want to be a part of this organization any longer or to be around these people who were caught in this rat race. There in that foul yard he had been better treated than he had ever been at any time in his life. 'They even love dogs,' he thought to himself.

The burly, hirsute guard was now bent on all his fours as he looked about in dismay and disbelief, because there was no hint of a dog in that room. A rat dashed across the storeroom and found a hiding place behind a carton of biscuits. The guard got off his feet in a start.

"Bloody sick rats! Is that what you feed people, rat droppings! I am sick of you." He was repulsed by the thought that the biscuits he had been sneaking from the pantry had been infested with rodents. The rat darted out of the door hoping all along that no one would see it. As luck would have it the guard spotted the rat and instead of chasing the ugly creature, he puked on the floor. The rat stopped in its tracks and stood wide-eyed looking at the vomit that had been thrown out with unusual force. The sound of expulsion, the splattering of the semi-solid, undigested remains of the food, and the grunt that followed the act had taken the little creature by surprise.

Sunderaman of pre-dog days would have hit the rat or at least chased it out but now he merely smiled.

"Are you all right brother? Why don't you go home, I will get someone to clean up around here," Sunderaman looked up from the rat to the guard and then down to the muck on the floor. The guard burst out into tears and the rat resumed its run out of the door.

After the guard left, Sunderaman got the bag of gems that had been left by Old Nick, out of its hiding place. He picked them up knowing that they would come to good use to feed the poor. "My life is about to change for the better," he said loudly to himself. He then went off to find Dr Amarjeet.

He found his doctor in the Gents.

Amarjeet was merrily humming a latest Bollywood number as his bladder relieved itself noisily in the dirty urinal. Sunderaman addressed him from behind.

"I have a friend who is not very well."

The doctor turned somewhat startled, "Why it is you, Sunderaman? You made me jump there; my you walk softly for a fat man. Wait, weren't you missing? Or had you gone away on long leave?"

"Kind of missing, yes. But right now I am here on urgent business. I have a friend, he is very ill. He is young and needs urgent medical attention. Can you come with me and perhaps help him?" asked Sunderaman.

"I will be happy to help but are you going to foot the bill for the treatment, Sunderaman?" asked the doctor as his eyebrow raised a little in wonder.

"I will pay whatever you want Dr Amarjeet."

"Are you sure, friend Sunderaman, do you have the funds?"

Sunderaman put his hand into his bag and plucked out a gemstone, he then handed it over to the good Dr Amarjeet. "Will this settle your greed?" he asked.

"No need for that kind of talk, my friend, because I am as much an employee here as you and your pantry boys. Even if I waive off my fees, I cannot pay your hospital bills. Look at the queues outside, there are not enough beds to accommodate free patients. I have no option but to admit your friend in the paid category, but bring your friend to the hospital and let me arrange for some concessions."

"No," replied Sunderaman, "I want you to come to his house and look after him there."

Dr. Amarjeet looked at the gemstone. "But?" he said.

"But me no buts, there are other doctors, Dr. Amarjeet, perhaps I will ask one of them."

Dr. Amarjeet looked at the fine gemstone as he replied, "No, no, I will come. I accept your offer. Just give me a few minutes to finish my duty hours. Don't worry about getting there, I will take you along on my motorcycle. After that we can have a jolly lunch at a *dhaba*."

So it was then that Sunderaman led the good Dr Amarjeet back to the house where the young boy was in need of treatment. Dr Amarjeet treated the boy and he was soon well and walking about. It was at this time that Dr Amarjeet saw the female dog that was about to give birth to its cubs and he stayed to help out with this also. It has to be said that Dr Amarjeet was so touched by the love and simplicity of the people living in that *slum* that he is now a regular visitor to this area and he visits for free.

Sunderaman had made himself known to the boy's father and it felt, that man said, as if he had known him forever. Sunderaman let the boy's father also know of the wealth that he had and proposed to contribute towards the welfare of the boy's family and the family of dogs, if he was allowed to rent a room in their house. The boy's father readily agreed and Sunderaman and he soon became very good friends.

REVELATIONS

∽

Yashoda looked out at the sea before her; she was surprised at how calm it was, and how it seemed to make her feel. As she looked she could sense that someone else was behind her, she could feel this somebody's eyes upon her. She turned slowly.

Chris smiled and as she looked, he seemed to radiate a kind of oneness, a happiness that could not be explained.

"Hello," said Yashoda in surprise, "we have met before I think."

"Hello, Yashoda, yes we have and now we meet again."

"I seem to remember that as soon as I got here you told me that you are my son's brother."

"Well, that at least is the truth, after all, we are all family in the sight of the one true God."

"And what God is this that you talk about?"

"Any God that you choose. In truth, God is one and the same to all things."

Yashoda thought for a moment.

"Now are you telling me that I was talking to a God some time ago? And that this God was the very devil. He turned me into a flower and then I died of thirst, it was not a pleasant death. But to me he was the son of the man who had betrayed me in my youth. That man had used my body for pleasure and discarded the fruit of my labour, my child. Oh my poor Krishna, now he is all alone in the world, alas my death has brought him much grief."

"I am pleased that you remember what happened as it saves me the trouble of lying to you, in a nice sort of welcoming way. Yes you died, and now you are here."

"And where is here?" asked Yashoda.

"This is heaven."

"Which one?"

"Why, mine."

"You don't look anything like Vishnu. And why aren't we floating on the clouds, and where are the other Gods? I mean your seniors," asked Yashoda.

"My seniors? Is that what Heaven looks like to you? Now there's some confusion, I mean you are in my heaven. This is not the sky and we are not floating here. See you can walk on your two feet, let's say things work a little differently out here. I am Christ but you can call me Chris."

"Christ! Oh no, no, no, you have got it all wrong. I don't belong here and that wicked brother of yours was no son of mine. And let me clarify that I am a devout Hindu, you have got me here by mistake. We need to set this right, and we need to do it right now."

"Surely no one is a Hindu or a Christian in the afterlife, once you die you leave those labels behind. You are not even a woman here, not in the way that you know or have known. We are all formless souls here, look at me, I am not any more tangible than you."

"Then why am I here?"

"In my religion we have an evil God, you have already met him. It was he that turned you into a flower; it was he that killed you. Krishna knows this and he has changed. He was once so placid and now he has changed; now he wants blood."

"Is that so wrong?"

"Yes it is, for Gods have no blood to give. You cannot kill a God. What he wants is wrong and he needs to be calmed down, for if his temper is let loose then it could be the end for all of us. When I say all of us, I mean every living thing could perish. Not just humans, but Gods also. Even the winds, even the rains, the sunshine, the snow, winter, spring, summer, autumn. Everything. It would all descend into chaos. If one God, even one such as Krishna, should err, then it is the end of everything and that is why you are here, Yashoda. This may come as a surprise. You have already been told that you are the mother of Krishna. Not just of Krishna but of the God Krishna made flesh. You are his Earthly mother and as such he is not going to let go that easily."

"I am no God's mother. I am just a mother of a human being and he is no God."

"You are our Lord Krishna's Earth mother, whether you like it or not. And he is a God."

"But he is just my son and now he is lonely in that wicked world. I just wish that he comes to no harm," and with these words Yashoda burst into tears. She turned then and looked back at the calming waves of the sea. Chris walked over and put his arms around her. When her tears had subsided, he went on to explain.

"This is my Heaven, all of us Gods have one. I was asked to look after you when you had passed on."

"But why?" asked Yashoda.

"Your religion is different from mine and when you pass, you go on almost straightaway to a new life; in my religion, souls stay a while. Krishna really is my brother and he will want to visit you before you move on to your next phase. I will look after you till he arrives. This heaven is very nice. You can take from it what you like. Everyone here is welcoming. Just enjoy your stay that is all."

"Are you trying to convert me?" asked the now smiling Yashoda.

"I am always after new followers," winked Chris as he started to fade.

"Wait, where are you going, what do I do next?"

Chris reappeared for a second and pointed at a building in the distance.

"Go to that building and ask for Alma, she will look after you for now. I have to go and see a man about a dog and also a few of my friends."

GODS REUNITED

༚

The Buddha had calmed Krishna in his own Godly way by transmitting calming electrons from his own electromagnetic field to Krishna's.

Buddy Roy had an extraordinarily high charge of certain electrons that made him contagiously calm. When he touched others or even as he spoke in his gentle voice, the charge in his body created ripples around his listener. It was as if the listener was drawn into Buddy Roy's electric field. Buddy's electrons permeated into others' nervous systems, triggering an electrochemical reaction in the hundred billion neurons. The calming impulse spread quickly, travelling through the connected dendrites of the neuron cells and stimulating the brain to produce calming hormones.

Krishna had walked into the sacred Ganges to bind himself with an oath to kill Old Nick. Buddha was worried because a resolve made in the sacred waters of the Ganges was binding and once bound by an oath, Krishna would either have to avenge his mother's death or kill himself. Buddy and Chris had left messages for Krishna on Facebook but Krishna had withdrawn into his own shell and disregarded their pleas. Left with no choice, Buddy Roy followed Krishna to Haridwar. He made himself appear on the extended pavement that led to the crowded *Har Ki Pauri*. Krishna knew nothing of Buddy's presence. The Buddha remained a few steps behind so as not to rouse Krishna's suspicion.

Even though Krishna was a God, and Gods know their destiny, he had been blocked out of the events that were to play out in the next one hour. Other Gods had had to block Krishna's prescience site in the brain. Fore knowledge or prescience is a cognitive trait given to Gods, saints, and some extraordinarily perceptive human beings. All human brains have some measure of this cognitive function, only most of us go through our lives without exploiting our latent talents and powers. Once this site, situated in the left hemisphere of the brain, is blocked or made dysfunctional, even Gods lose their sixth sense.

Unaware of the trick that had been played upon him by fellow Gods, Krishna had arrived in the holy city of Haridwar. It was a languid hour before evening and most people were either asleep or watching and waiting for their evening cup of tea at tea-stalls off the pavement. Krishna went looking for a barber to shave his head before going to the *Gau Ghat* for a dip.

"It's time for tea. You won't find any barber at this hour. I won't be long," he informed Krishna. As an afterthought, he added, "Why don't you have some tea, brother?"

"It will warm you brother, after the dip you will feel the chill of your loss. My mother always said that even in the fierce, relentless summer the Ganga is cool and fresh. It does not warm up to our woes, friend. Don't push yourself too hard, you cannot go with the dead," the tea-stall owner pitched in.

As is the tradition in India, more so in the pilgrimage towns, people talk to each other without any introduction. They go on to reveal secrets, pour their woes to a kind ear and hear of others' tragedies. After half an hour of talk at the tea-stall, the barber guided Krishna to his shop and shaved his head with an unsterile razor blade. Krishna flinched at the sight of the razor that had been washed in soapy water; it had collected rust stains over time and use. But it was a custom in Hinduism to have the head shaved at a barber's after performing the last rites of the dead. His best bet was to have brought a fresh blade, but it was a minute too late.

"Have you come all alone brother?" asked the barber who believed it was his right to know something about the people he served.

'Alone, are we ever alone in this country?' thought Krishna to himself. 'If only we could be alone, that would be a true wonder to behold.'

Krishna had an hour's wait before sunset, the hour he had chosen to take the vow. So he rested on a concrete bench on the pavement. Every few minutes someone would come by to sell him flowers, or a pack of incense sticks, or sacred beads or some other symbol of Hinduism. Krishna had turned laconic and angry after his mother's death and social company was the last thing he needed. He decided to walk to the quieter banks of *Gau Ghat* instead of using a Godly way to make himself appear everywhere. He walked self-absorbed and thinking out his plan when a monk brushed past him. Their shoulders touched for a second and their forearms rubbed against one another with a mystical force. Krishna felt a strange electric field surround him but he chose to ignore it.

Buddy Roy's electric charge soon took over Krishna and when he reached the *ghat,* he knew a force other than his own had been worked at him. He descended the steps at the *ghat* calmly, thinking only of his mother's love. When he stood in the waters he remembered his mother's tears. Her life's struggles flashed before him. He then looked at the sky and bid his farewell in the cool waters of the mother river.

The calming waters of the Ganges caressed him tenderly. The ripples nursed his wounds. The noise, the soft-slapping noises were soothing too. When the sun settles on the water and reflects its heat that too is calming. Even in the darkness of the night, the Ganges has a calming effect. In the darkness, as the moon shines down from above, there is calmness.

But at this time as the shaven-headed Krishna, under Buddy Roy's influence, looked down at the cooling waters, he felt the calmness of the Ganges as the water wrapped itself around him. And as the water wrapped around him, so did its calming energies.

He soaked for a while with his eyes closed as he enjoyed the feelings that were now around him. After a short while he opened his eyes as he felt himself refreshed and then gazed at his reflection in the water. His hair was growing back. Krishna smiled to himself as he watched, he had been bald for a while but now his hair was growing. Before long it was back to its original glory, flowing down and resting upon his shoulders.

"I could be looking at a picture of Chris himself," said Krishna as he glared at his reflection.

The God Krishna stood then in silence as he soaked his skin in the waters. He then relaxed and fell back and floated on top of the river, smiling.

Sometime later after he had soaked up all its calming effect, he opened his eyes and saw the Buddha floating before him.

"Do you see now, my young brother, do you see what it is all about?"

Krishna smiled as he relaxed and then winked knowingly to his fellow God.

LIGHT AND DARK

৪১

Buddy Roy, the Buddha, had not only been active in the Krishna department, he had also been keeping an eye on the other Gods. Little did they know that he had been entrusted with certain promises from a long lost God.

He had seen to it that Chris had taken care of Krishna's mother, for surely he would want to see her one last time. He had also pacified many of the lesser Gods who were still on the path of evolution. He had become adept at building computer programs and was very fond of the virtual worlds that could be built if you had enough memory space within the computer. He knew that these virtual worlds in this new realm that was known as cyberspace could be vast, almost as vast as the very heavens that he had known for so long now.

As he tinkered with his little foibles of this new technology, he thought of his friends and what kind of geeks they were. Chris had fallen behind in discovering internet, but once he logged into it he became hooked.

Friendships were one thing but existence had to carry on, this he knew and also that he had a job to perform and remain loyal to his own beliefs.

The Buddha settled down in his thoughts and then manifested himself elsewhere. It was here that he had made himself known to the God known as Old Nick and this is how the conversation went.

"It looks as if you have won then Nick, Christ is in turmoil and Krishna is at this very moment dying in the Ganges and has absolutely no chance of getting out of its sucking fetid foulness. He will die soon and you will have won this battle, you could of course save him, should you wish to."

"Save Krishna, why would I want to do that?" asked Nick. "What has he done for me? He only upsets me. Some brother he has been. No, let him die and I will then reign supreme."

"If you do not save him, then who will you fight in the future?"

"I do not need or wish to fight any one God, I just want to reign supreme, fresh in the knowledge that all the others recognize me as the Supreme Being."

"That will never happen, surely you know this," said Buddy Roy as he sank towards the Earth a little, with a loss of concentration over his levitation.

"You are losing your faith Buddha, you sink a little."

"A mere moment's lack of concentration, see I have regained my composure," replied Buddy Roy as he floated freely again.

"You are worried, are you not? You know that should I win this battle that you too will have to bow down before me."

"Nick, we were all created as equals, we are all made of the same clay from the same kilns. Why would you want to rise above your station?"

"Someone has to lead; someone has to be held in awe above the rest, otherwise all will be chaos."

"But we do not need this. We should all be equal."

"If I cannot be the leader then I will make sure that the heavens fall and all will become chaos," said Old Nick, the Devil.

The Buddha looked at Old Nick and smiled as he said, "So be it then Nick, you have my blessing and my obedience." And as he said these words, he made a few signs with his hands and then faded into nothingness. Only to reappear instantly in front of Nick again.

"I have checked in the Ganges, Master," said Buddy Roy to Old Nick. "Krishna is dead, I saw his body as it floated on the waters, his bald head bobbed about face-down and without life; he is dead for sure! What are we to do next, Master?"

Old Nick smiled. 'So I have won then,' he thought. "All right Roy, I want you to go to Chris next and ask that he joins with me or I will let loose chaos."

"It will be done, Master," replied the Buddha who then disappeared and in an instant reappeared.

"It took some doing," said the Buddha, "but he has readily agreed to bow down and worship you."

"This is more like it," roared Old Nick as he continued giving orders and created havoc as he went from God to God.

All Gods followed him now. Nick was happy as he brought happiness to himself and suffering to everyone and everything else.

In his rule, he soon got tired of Buddy Roy and banished him to a non-gravity world where he could not float no matter how hard he tried.

Christ was also made to suffer as he made him a doctor in a hospice where he could not help the dying no matter how hard he tried.

Krishna was brought back to life and was made to watch the death of his Earthly Mother over and over again.

Old Nick, the Devil, revelled in his victory and was as happy as he could be in the world where he was the Supreme Being.

WINDOWS, TO VERY SOUL OF LIFE

୫୦

All the computers were taken up when Krishna reached the cyber cafe at noon. He had been thinking of getting himself a laptop of late. The wait at Internet cafes was beginning to eat into his Godly task time and as much as he enjoyed his gossip hour at the cyber stations, there were Godly things that could not be ignored. He had lost the luxury of using the computer in the doctors' room at the hospital ever since he had taken off to Japan and lost his job as a pantry boy.

As he stood waiting for his turn to use the computer, he heard Sunderaman's voice over the din of the traffic outside the shop. He followed Sunderaman's voice into the cafe, and there he was, talking to the computer, his head moving vigorously in a convulsive involuntary motion. Sunderaman struggled to juggle with the icons on the top of his mail inbox. He had deleted an important mail by mistake. Krishna chuckled and thought to himself, 'But if I get a laptop I will miss all the fun of meeting human beings.'

"What noise you make, Sunderaman! Are you voice chatting or something?" Krishna patted Sunderaman's bulky shoulders. However much Sunderaman tried, he could not get that flab off himself.

"Krishna! Can you retrieve my mail, I have trashed it by mistake, it's all so messy you know," Sunderaman handed his work station to Krishna.

Krishna restored the mail from the trash in a jiffy, with a touch of a key, as Sunderaman stood baffled.

"Here you go, Sunderaman. How are you?" Krishna stepped aside to face him.

"I---Oh! I am so sorry, how are you my brother? I forgot all about it, where have you been? I learnt about your mother. I came visiting with the other boys but you had left for Haridwar. We were all there, Raju, Sukhram and the other boys. Why didn't you inform us Krishna? You don't consider us your own?"

Sunderaman pulled Krishna to his burly chest and embraced him tight. Krishna returned the bear hug with warm affection and pondered over the love of these poor earthlings who made brothers out of colleagues and friends out of strangers.

"I am sorry but the turn of events was such, my brother. I am touched by your gesture. How are the other boys? Aren't you supposed to be at the hospital at this hour?" Krishna put his arm around Sunderaman's shoulder.

"Shhh!" came someone's voice.

"What Shhh man? We all work here in the midst of chaos and noise! If you want absolute quiet then go buy yourself a computer!" Sunderaman had still not got out of his habit of making facetious remarks at anyone who differed with him. Krishna, the omniscient, winked at the boy who had challenged Sunderaman.

"Come brother, let's catch up over a cup of tea. A cosy tea-stall has come up round the corner; let's chat under the cool of the banyan tree, my friend, and maybe we can feast on *samosas* as well."

Krishna led Sunderaman out of the cafe to the banyan tree where a new tea joint had sprouted out of nowhere. Temples and food joints needed no permit or license in the poor suburbs of the city; they simply started their business anywhere and got away by paying petty bribes to the local policemen.

The new tea joint was tucked in a narrow bylane, off the main road, but not too far from the local shops. Within a week of starting out, the tea-stall had built a network of dedicated clients who ordered several rounds of tea during their long business hours. The delivery boy, a lad of no more than ten, ran around the shops with small glasses of tea firmly placed in the glass-holder, and a notebook tucked under his armpit. After an hour he returned to collect the empty glasses and take down the order for the next round of tea. The business ran on weekly credit; all the dues were settled at the end of the week and the records were maintained in a notebook, which the clients had to sign upon the delivery of tea.

"So you have found yourself a new life, Sunderaman. But what about your wife and children, why should you abandon them?" Krishna observed after Sunderaman had narrated his story.

"Don't even mention them; they didn't miss me when I was gone. They went about claiming a life-insurance! Can you believe it? They are paid every month for my death! The ungrateful lot! I spent all my life looking after their needs and this is what they did to me." Sunderaman devoured the *samosas* and ordered a plate of *kachodis*.

"Don't you think you need to cut down on fried snacks? Maybe you would like to see yourself leaner?"

Krishna looked at the empty glass of tea that he held in his long hands. "Hey uncle, you make such good tea here! But it's so unfair to charge five rupees for 100 ml of tea!" Krishna turned to the owner of the tea-stall, who was the sole proprietor and the cook of the *dhaba*. The man twitched his gaunt face at the mention of money; he flicked his hair back to its position before coming up with an answer. His hair had turned orange from applying henna to camouflage the greys. His beard too had a tinge of orange, but it was mostly black because it had not been coloured for as long as the hair on his head. He opened his mouth to reveal the mottled teeth with beetle stains on them, and then he lowered the flame of the stove, allowing the *kachodis* to turn a golden brown on a slow flame. After spitting out the remains of the beetle leaf that he had been chewing, he addressed his customers.

"Elder brother, now be fair in your judgement," he started by addressing Sunderaman. "This friend of yours is a young boy, what does he know? In the last year alone, the grocery prices have risen by 50 per cent or more; is that not so? Since you get home groceries and all, you have got to know. And what does the government say? It is driven by outside forces! I ask you brother, what is this outside force? Who is this outside force? I am not educated like you, elder brother, I may be a humble illiterate fool, but mind you, this government cannot fool the likes of me."

Sunderaman nodded in appreciation, for he had been addressed with deference and referred to as educated.

"We are all the same, brother. A high school certificate means nothing. I didn't go to any university, but I am better informed than any double M.A. on most things. You are a fount of knowledge yourself. No one needs degrees to understand life's problems. Look at the corruption, scams, underworld mafia-politician nexus that brought our country to this state? Why, it's the guys with college degrees and money – who else? Do you think a poor, illiterate man can count the money these guys make on deals? I don't know how many zeros you write in one million. Look at the money the rich have – millions or maybe trillions! It never gets hard on them, but the poor have to shrink their meals further. Our wages remain obsolete and paltry. But the inflation is alike for the rich and the poor. I sympathize with you, brother." Sunderaman spoke with a grim expression, recalling whatever he could of the news analysis on television.

"What a gentleman you are, brother. The next cup of tea is on me," the tea-stall owner was touched by the affection that the fat man gave him.

For a while they discussed corrupt politicians and inflation and then the talk drifted to Sunderaman's new family.

"I say Krishna, move in with me. These people are family to me. They will take you in." Then he whispered to Krishna, "Don't worry, I have enough money to see us through." The mention of money reminded Krishna of Nick and his own mother who was in Heavenly Clacton with Christ at the moment.

"Now listen Sunderaman, I don't have time, I have to leave for some place soon. And you are doing well, my brother, but don't be mean to your family. Go back to them and you can still be of help to this new set of people you love. We cannot escape our responsibilities, it is wrong. Give my love to all the pantry-boys and convey my regards to all your girlfriends," Krishna nudged Sunderaman to indicate that a special nurse had been referred to.

"Nurses? Oh yes, now that you mention it, Shiny has left for the US. She found a job." Even though Sunderaman had changed his ways, somewhere a part of him yearned for Shiny. He was reminded of his pain and he turned quiet at the reminder of his lost love.

"Go back to your people, Sunderaman, for your own sake. Our desires are insatiable that is why nature cannot bestow its bounty on everyone. Shiny is not yours, you may love her though; but what is yours is your wife and children, own them up." Krishna handed the empty plates and glasses to the errand boy, who had just returned after delivering the morning tea to his master's customers. Though small in size, the boy was sharp and brisk; within minutes he was done with the dishes. Krishna was reminded of his own childhood as an errand boy at a sweet shop.

"Hey lad, where do you live?" Krishna asked.

"Not far," the boy was laconic or perhaps afraid to talk in his master's presence. Krishna turned to Sunderaman, "Are you returning to the cyber cafe?"

"Why, yes. I had to reply to Sister Joana's mail. She wants me to arrange accommodation for a friend of hers. I have so much on my plate, Krishna, I must have been God's special child for him to have saddled me with so many responsibilities."

They started walking back to the cyber cafe.

"Oh that you are, Sunderaman. I can tell you, you are God's special son." He laughed and squeezed Sunderaman's shoulders. "But what is this thing about Joana, tell me buddy?"

"How did you miss this? You won't believe what people are up to these days Krishna! Remember I told you about the Facebook thing once, the day you got angry with me. Now this whole Facebook business has made lovers out of old people. There's this man who comes down from a foreign country to meet Joana. She introduces him as a Facebook friend to the world, but my word Krishna, she has hitched up with someone at last." Sunderaman winked and clapped his plump hands as he narrated Joana's story.

"And she asks you to arrange his lodging and all?" Krishna probed further.

"Krishna, what can I say about myself, my boy? I love helping people; it's my self-appointed role these days. Poor woman, she needs some sort of a companion in life. It gives me happiness to help others, and that fellow is quite a gentleman. I like him."

Sunderaman approved of Joanna's choice and elaborated on the many uses of Facebook. Before they could reach the shop, an old acquaintance of Sunderaman's ran into them.

"Hey Sunderaman, my friend; where have you been these days? I am in trouble, brother; I need to shift into a new house. My landlord has served us an eviction order! Can you help me find another place?"

"Krishna, my lad, you go your way then. See, what did I tell you about being saddled with responsibilities? I will call Joana later in the day; let me go and help this brother of mine. His need is urgent; I must cut you short, my brother. But I will catch you later and don't you vanish this time. And yes, I have been thinking about what you said, I will accept your good advice and meet my family soon." Sunderaman vanished into a labyrinth of lanes and Krishna walked down to the cyber cafe.

In his Facebook message box there was a reminder from Chris:

Hello Krishna. Be assured that Yashoda is looked after and rested. She is trying to make meaning out of the life that she lived. We spend our evenings together and I may add she has quite taken to English tea and scones. Mind you mate, never have scones without whipped cream and jam. Your mother finds the whole thing scrumptious! Come and see her soon, so that she may go on with her journey. Btw, Buddy Roy is handling Nick, don't feel distressed on that account. See you soon mate. Chris.

Krishna read the message over and over again, he thought of his mother's life and what she could have deciphered from it. She was too simple in her mind to draw inferences from experiences, but her faith in goodness and God was firm and unflinching. 'At least she is happy, somewhere, in some form,' he said to himself and logged off.

He paid 30 rupees at the reception of the Internet café to a man who could not spell the word computer right. In India people used technology, even earned money from it, without any training or knowhow of the technology they put to use.

He walked back to the house where he had lived with his mother. He felt drawn to his childhood, though as a God he was not bound by time and age. He spent some quiet moments, meditating and humming celestial sounds.

Then he faded as he went to find his future.

GOD AND HIS MOTHER

৪৩

It was warm here, a summer's day. The man with the long hair smiled as he looked up. Not into the sun. No, he just looked heavenwards and smiled as the sun radiated down on his face.

He was quite tall and had long black hair that fell onto his shoulders. He had a smile that radiated warmth and happiness. He squatted down for a moment and took into his hand warm sand and as he looked out at the sea, he let the sand slip through his fingers. 'It is quite, quite beautiful here,' he thought.

"Yes, it is very beautiful here," came a voice in agreement.

Krishna stood up and said as he turned, "Hello, brother, it has been a long time."

"Too long brother," replied Chris."

These two young Gods hugged each other tight. It was a fond welcome and they once again felt as if they were but one being. These two were once again in harmony with each other. They walked together and chatted for hours. Chris explained this little piece of heaven that he had made and how it worked. Krishna listened avidly and said that he too might well go along these lines of a transit station between lives. Then of course they argued about the meaning of life and death and of what follows after. After all, even Gods are flawed and human.

Eventually though, the conversation turned to Yashoda.

"How is my mother?" asked Krishna.

"She is as well as can be expected, she was not expecting this, though. As you well know, she was brought up to respect your religion and this is quite hard for her to understand. She knows that she is dead but cannot understand why she has not been carried forward to her next incarnation. This religion of yours does baffle me at times, brother."

"So can I go and talk to her?"

"Why yes."

"And you have no objections to me helping her on her journey to the next life, if that's what she wants?"

"Of course not, she is your Earthly mother and if it is your religion that she wishes to follow, then so be it."

"I thought that I would ask, brother, after all this is your heaven."

"All are welcome here, even as guests."

"Thank you for all that you have done," said Krishna, "I will go and settle things with my mother and after that we will have to talk about what we are going to do about our other brother, Old Nick himself."

The Christ watched as Krishna walked down the beach in search of his mother. Chris had never really expected this moment to come. To see his brother here in his own kingdom of heaven was a wonder in itself. Chris smiled and as he smiled, the sun above seemed to radiate even more warmth.

Krishna walked along the beach admiring the scenery and enjoying the sunshine. Sometime later as he was walking towards a cottage, he saw a woman hanging out her washing on the line. He marveled at the contours of her body as only a child looking at his mother can. "Mother!" he shouted in happiness as he ran towards her.

Yashoda turned and saw the young man running towards her. She smiled as only a mother can when she sees her son for the first time in ages. Krishna picked his mother up and turned in circles, laughing and shouting with joy. At last these two had found each other for the last time.

"Krishna, you naughty boy, put me down, people will see us, what will they think, and where have you been, and why did you not tell me that you were the Lord God Krishna incarnate?" His mother went on and on with her prattling as Krishna held her aloft and spun round and round in happiness. At last he calmed down and let his mother fall to her feet. He kissed her forehead and then one by one he took her hands in his, they were worn and wrinkled from Earthly toil. He kissed them and wept, for these hands had laboured day and night for his sake. After he had wept a long time, he smiled at her as only the Lord God Krishna can, but then his smile diminished a little into the smile that Yashoda recognized of her little boy.

"Oh Krishna, it is so good to see you again, let me look at my boy."

Krishna stood apart from his Earthly mother as she stared at him, not only in wonder but also in motherly love.

"Mother, I had to come and see you. I love you so much."

"And I have always loved you like a mother, what should I say, God?"

"Forget the God thing for now, we are just family at this moment."

"Just family you say?" asked the mother.

"That's right mother."

Yashoda drew back her arm and slapped the boy around the face. "Then where have you been, how could you let your mother suffer so? No son would ever allow his mother to suffer as I have suffered, you say that you love me but you have been negligent. How I have suffered and all this time my son was a God!"

"Mother, I am sorry but it is just the way of things. Your suffering is your *karma*, you are not above *karma* for being my mother. I cannot change that, but I chose you over others to be my mother; why would I do that? Because I wanted to ease your suffering, so that I could partake of it, and be by your side whenever there was a need."

"So you return to me now, I am dead you know! Your so-called brother, Chris, has explained his heaven to me and now you turn up to do what? Can you make me happy in the next life? Can you compensate for the woes of this life? Oh how I had yearned for one man and he was not given to me! Why did you have to be his seed?"

"Mother, it really does not matter what I can or cannot do. It is of no consequence what was given and what was taken away. All that matters is that at this moment we are together again."

"But that's it, it is just a moment."

"Mother, you do not realize this but in heaven, any heaven, any limbo, any afterlife where we wait to be reborn, a moment can last a lifetime; an eternity always to be revisited whenever you wish."

"But," uttered Yashoda.

"No buts, mother, let's wander through eternity for a moment or two and then we will talk some more." So it was that Krishna disappeared with his Earthly Mother to explain and experience the intricacies of life, the universe, and existence itself.

Sometimes a lifetime can appear to last for just a moment. It can appear to go so fast and in an instant it seems that it has gone. Sometimes an instant can seem to last forever, or a lifetime may pass in an instant.

The sun was setting on the little heaven that is Clacton-on-Sea as the two of them returned from their travels. During these travels (which had indeed taken a lifetime), Yashoda and her son Krishna had come to know each other once again. The love that they now shared spanned not only family love but also godliness itself.

"So here we are then, mother," said Lord Krishna, "are you ready to move forward?"

Yashoda looked at her God and as she looked at him, she also saw her son. "Son," she said, "I am as proud as any mother can be of her son. As your devotee I am awed by what I have seen and understood of Cosmos. You have shown me the way, and on this way I will find salvation from this cycle of births and deaths. I am now ready to move forward to my new life and promise me son, this will be my last life. As much as I would have wanted you for a son again, I will not press for it. You may cut the cords between us."

"The cords will remain, because these are the cords of the Universe. Do you think that I will not come to see you again in your new life?"

"But will I know you?"

"You will know, you will always know, the love goes with you and it clings. It is not only the atoms that bind a body but the love of all others too."

"Thank you Krishna for being the son that you have been and for being Lord Krishna himself. I am ready now, give my love to your brothers, to all of them, including Old Nick, for he is just a cog in the wheel of this great big existence that we all share."

"Spoken like a God's mother, I always knew that you would see it and understand the mysteries of the Universe. Now you move to your last life as a realized soul, a soul that knows it all and lives in that knowledge given to the sages alone."

Krishna stood on the beach as he watched his mother fade. He knew that she could not have stayed much longer in Christ's heaven and she had to go forward and follow her own faith, her own destiny, if you will.

Krishna stood on the beach alone now. Alone as he looked out towards the sea. 'A poem would be in order,' he thought.

The sea, it rolls
It rolls like thunder
It pulls you in
It makes you wonder
The waves they crash
They crash and they die
One moment angry they seem
Then calm, they lie

The air it rages
As the storm flits about
Then calms once again
As the tides they go out
Like humans the waves grow
And live to their full extent
Then crash into nothingness
Their life song almost spent
But there is always one thing
The soul travels on
For without this spark
We would all be gone.

Krishna recited his poem and then consigned it to the deep as he looked out onto the vista before him.

"Beautiful sentiments, brother, I am sorry but I heard your private poem," said Chris quietly, who now stood beside him.

Krishna smiled as he turned. "It is of no consequence, brother, it was such a small thing."

"It was no small thing, are you sad now?" asked Chris.

"No, I have bonded deeply with mother, better than we bonded as living beings. In a way I should thank Old Nick if I ever see him again, for without him, perhaps I would never have had this time with my mother."

"Our existence is very strange, is it not?"

"Strange indeed, brother, but what of Old Nick, should we chase him, should we try to wreak our vengeance upon him?"

"What do you think?"

"What do you both think and what do you want?" asked the Buddha as he appeared beside them. He was almost perfect in his floating now and had achieved a four-foot float above the ground.

"Hello Roy," said the two Gods.

"Well then, what are we to do about Nicky?"

"What can we do Roy?" asked Krishna in reply.

"Yes, what can we do, he is as much a part of us as we are of him. One day he will come back and make our lives hell again though, won't he?"

Buddy Roy, the Buddha, looked at his two friends and said,

"Well, not for some time. You see I have been working on a new project and I have studied the computer network and cyberspace. I have become very skilful at computer programming and I have built a virtual world where even at this moment Old Nick has been placed and is the king. He rules this chaotic kingdom in his own way and he is immensely happy. We are all there in this computer-generated world; there is a virtual Buddy Roy, who even at this moment is calling him Master, and there's a virtual Krishna and a virtual Chris. We are all there in his world and he is quite, quite happy as he rules us with a heavy rod."

"But surely, he must know that it is just a computer program, Roy."

"Well if he does, then he has not said so, so far, and he seems to be happy in there. I would let you look in but he would sense your presence and that might prove to be a disaster. So for now, let's just leave him in his happiness and hope that he stays where he is. We can go back to our worlds now."

"Buddy Roy, you are a genius," said Chris as they walked along the beach.

"I have to say that I totally agree with Chris," said the Lord Krishna.

"Well, there is a first," said the Buddha with a smile, "Gods agreeing with each other."

PARTY ON

꧁

The world moved on a little as indeed it tended to do.. The Buddha went back to his own region and religion. He sent out the electric charge to spread peace around.

The Lord Krishna also returned to his own place and looked over his followers. He did what he could to alleviate the sufferings of the Third World, in a detached, amused way.

Chris, of course, continued in his own way as he looked after his flock, one minute in his private heaven and then off to another dimension of reality, space and time on Earth.

A date had been set though and this date was for some unexplained reason April 26. This was the date that the first Gods' convention would be held. It had been arranged that this first convention would take place in Chris's kingdom of heaven.

And so it was that on April 26, the first act stood upon the stage carrying out a sound check. This stage even now floated out on the waters of the sea, out before the Heavenly Clacton-on-Sea.

On the beach, table after table had been laid out with food, for all tastes of course. Some of the greatest chefs ever to have lived (and died and now lived on in this afterlife) had been invited to attend and to make as sumptuous a feast as possible.

Chris had done a fine job of inviting all the old Gods and friends that he knew that Krishna would love to see again. All the Gods were there.

"What is the party for?" asked one God, "it is not your birthday, is it?"

"No," replied Krishna, "it is just that Chris wanted to honour me for some reason or the other."

"Well I hope that he is going to organize a party like this for me sometime," said another God.

"Well Chris, will you be honouring all Gods like this in the future?" asked the God known as the Little Old Man.

Chris smiled, "I have known my brother Krishna for my entire existence. I wanted to celebrate our friendship, to honour him for being the God that he is. Show me a God as charmingly clever and humanly passionate as him. He has been a friend extraordinaire, a co-traveller across time and space; we need to celebrate our unique friendship. After all it is just a party and although I name it in his honour, it is really for all of us to enjoy."

The Little Old Man smiled as he went off to look at the tables upon tables of food that had been laid out.

"I hope that the food will not be wasted brother," said Krishna to Chris as he sat down on the beach beside him.

"Oh hello brother, no, the food will not be wasted, I am even now arranging a reverse famine to occur on Earth."

"That sounds an interesting theory, how will it work?"

"As it always has, brother, I will make sure that next year, an adequate amount of sunshine is shone down and that all the harvests will be abundant and good all over the world."

"You are a benevolent God, my friend."

"The party will start soon Krishna, are you looking forward to the music?"

"I am happy to say that I am, it will take our minds away from our usual problems. How wise of you to allow us all a sideshow from our usual lives."

"Not I, we. For all Gods must surely be in agreement for this to happen."

"We must have all willed it," Krishna turned to look at the gleeful Gods.

"What of your mother?" asked Chris.

Krishna looked at him as if in thought for a moment, "Perhaps we will speak of that at a later date, for now let's just enjoy the music and let our souls fly."

"Have you tried the chips, chap?" Chris asked Krishna.

"They are somewhat bland, I am not at all sure that I like them."

"Here," said Chris as he passed his brother a bowl of chips, "take one and dip it into this locally made curry sauce, you will love it."

Krishna took the chip and then dunked it into the curry sauce and then ate it. "Mmmm!" said the God, "not bad. I didn't know you liked hot sauces!"

"With those many Indian restaurants in England we have had a change of palette, my friend," Chris chuckled.

The festivities continued and then the first band appeared on stage.

"You will like this," said Chris.

"That's George Harrison, isn't it?" asked Krishna.

"It is indeed."

"He is one of mine now, brother, you know that?"

Chris smiled as the show began.

"Hello Clacton!" shouted out the singer George Harrison. "Here is my new band, the Eternal Travelling Willburreys! And boy have we travelled! On guitar, John Lennon, on sitar, Ravi Shankar, on guitar, Roy Orbison and guesting for this one show only, Elvis Presley himself!"

The crowd went wild as the stars started to belt out the first song, "Give Me Love," a classic Harrison tune.

The Buddha sat on the beach before them (that is to say he floated a few feet above the sands). He enjoyed himself, smiling silently.

"How have you arranged this Chris, George died some time ago and has been reborn and is now a taxi driver in London," said Krishna.

"I had a word with Buddy Roy, he arranged some sort of time shift. George is here just after he died, just for this one show, you understand?"

"Well not really but it is a great show all the same."

Next up was Karen Carpenter singing, "I'm on the Top of the World."

Krishna smiled, as did Chris and all the other Gods. As the songs continued, so did the love. It permeated around all those in attendance. More and more music was played and every God in attendance enjoyed the show and as some of them danced, so fire and lightning emanated from their beings, adding to the ongoing cacophony. With the Gods enjoying themselves, the show became even greater. Beautiful colours could be seen all over the waters and the lands and as each song and musical recital came to an end, a sense of peace and well-being came over this little heaven that was known as Clacton-on-Sea.

Beautiful colours of the deepest pastel shades of green and blue, tinged with reds and yellows and then the blazing oranges and deepest pinks. The sky lit up and shone as if the very sky itself was as happy as happy could be.

Then as if to heighten the effect, thunder started to clap in the sky as lightning flashed in unison with certain chords that were struck on the instruments that the musicians played. The Gods smiled and clapped along with the show, the music and the effects. Chris took a sly look at Buddy Roy and noticing that he was smiling broadly, he too beamed brightly.

Krishna looked at Chris and smiled as he pointed out other little wonders, "Look at that beautiful colour that is even now rising out on the waves."

"Could we ask for anything more, mate?" asked Chris.

"This is so beautiful, you were right my friend, it is about time that we all came together and rejoiced in this bounty that we have been given, for it is a wonder to behold, even without the music and the Gods, the Earth is still a wondrous place."

"Indeed my friend, Gods or no Gods Earth is a beautiful planet."

"Well-spoken brother. And for your sake, Kumar Gandharv has been brought back from his state of salvation. He sings even after attaining salvation, you know. And from what I know his voice is now the celestial sound, the sound of cosmic particles vibrating. I bet you will enjoy this part of the show. The greats together and 'live'. There's that very special wine from Italy's vineyards, you must drink plenty today Krishna, I insist. We have had such an eventful year together, brother. Let's rejoice in the peace that prevails." Chris was ebullient like a child eager to share his toys with a new friend.

"Peace! Yes, this unrest around the world is only a step towards greater world peace." Krishna winked at Christ who had been baffled by the Occupy Movements all over the world. He knew Krishna had read his mind and offered an indirect hint for an answer.

The show continued into the night. Then came, a great fireworks show as the Gods got drunk and got happy. Much enjoyment was had right up till the end of the show. As the two Gods, Chris and Krishna now walked along the beach together arm in arm, Krishna said, "Let's drink to the peace to come, my friend. But where are my fellow Hindu Gods?"

"They are at the bar, brother! Where else will Gods be? Come, let's join them!"

"And who are these dancing women with veils on their faces?"

"Krishna, they are those women who had men dancing around them all their lives! Ha, ha, now they have to compensate by dancing for others. Why, maybe you know a couple of them yourself? Look closely, they are all celebrated actresses of yesteryears. Their faces are veiled because their beauty has been taken from them with the passage of time. There's only a hint of their former selves now."

"Ah, now I see. Is that not Greta Garbo, how plain she looks now and yes, humbled. The cyclical nature of universe," Krishna considered the faces of guests and entertainers that surrounded him.

"Is that Michael Jackson that I see there, gosh? Why, you have turned him around with love and food, he looks so much better with those layers of fat on him. Is that some sort of reversal too, brother? But we cannot have this, for this one night surely all must be at their best," and with these words Krishna snapped his fingers and all the yesteryears faded, and yesterday's stars suddenly reverted to the best appearance that they had had when they were alive.

"Happiness must abound, Lord."

"I totally agree, Lord," came the reply.

The Gods continued with their partying through the night. Much food was eaten and much wine was drunk. Everyone in heaven was happy. Plush sofas, exquisite lacquer furniture, fine silk curtains, hand-embroidered cotton lace hemmed to the white table covers, crystal glasses and silver platters, neon lights and pyrotechnic display, music and dancing damsels, food and wine; the whole affair was splendidly opulent and breathtakingly grand. The Gods went back to their own kingdoms afterwards thinking that it was the best party in a few thousand years.

And this happiness was so big that it was felt on Earth itself.

Everything in the Garden of Eden as on the Earth was indeed rosy.

The next morning, in the Heavenly Kingdom of Clacton-on-Sea, Chris stood on the beach as he looked out to the sea. Beside him, dug into the sand was his fishing rod, the line from it stretched out far into the sea where it had been cast. He was happy now and watched intently towards the end of his line in the hope that he would catch a very large fish.

"Good morning, brother," came a voice from behind.

"Hello Krishna," he replied as he turned and looked at the approaching figure.

"Any luck?" asked Krishna as he pointed at the line.

"Not yet my friend, but I am hopeful, patience is after all a virtue."

Krishna smiled and then said, "It was a good night, that's for sure."

"It was indeed and I hope that in a way it has brought us all a little bit closer together."

"Oh I am sure that it has, look you have a bite."

Chris grabbed at his rod and started to reel in the caught fish. As this beast was landed he put his foot on its head and said, "Don't just stand their brother, bash its brains in."

Krishna looked at Chris and then knelt down and took the fish from under his brother's foot. He unhooked the hook from the fish's mouth and then picking it up in his hands carried it out into the sea where he let it go. To swim off and have another go at life.

"We all deserve a second chance, brother," said he to Chris with a smile.

Chris returned the smile, "We all have lessons to learn, brother."

The two of them sat for a while on the beach talking. Eventually Chris asked once again about Yashoda.

"The thing is Chris, in my religion, the souls go on, they are reborn. I was fortunate that you gave me the time with her but eventually, she had to go on. Though, I can visit her in her next birth, should I want."

"Is she the same person though, brother?"

Krishna looked at his brother and replied, "She is certainly the same soul, let's leave it there, for now, my friend."

For the rest of the day these two old friends sat and looked out to the sea, happy in each other's company. But time moves on, as it normally does, and eventually they stood on the beach as they faced each other and said their goodbyes.

"It has been fun, brother," said one.

"Yes I so hope that we can do it again next year."

"This Internet thing is a wondrous invention; let's make sure that we stay in touch."

"Yes, man has created such wonderful worlds, even though they are virtual. Only if he had remained pure in his soul," Krishna said with disappointment.

"He will come around one day, brother. Let's believe in him," Chris said with some cheer in his voice. The two of them hugged each other and then just disappeared into nothingness.

The nothingness of their own worlds, that is.

ROSE

⮞⮜

Yashoda returned to another place in another life and another time. A much happier and blessed life she was given; a life, that was perhaps, watched over by Gods.

Yashoda was reborn in the city of London in the year 2020. Her parents had come to this great land in search of happiness and wealth; the very reasons that impel men to abandon their homes and settle in foreign lands. Her father was an accountant out of instinct and not training, and her mother had a small flower shop in a downtown suburb of London. They were middle class Londoners, first-generation settlers, who had moved up the rung of the social ladder through dint of hard work and dogged persistence.

Their home decor was more English than Indian. All the 'God' icons, a salient feature of Hindu households, had been relegated to a corner, away from the sight of visitors. Ornate Victorian candelabras adorned the fireplace next to the bar. The featured walls in all the rooms displayed their smiling photos to give the impression of a happy marriage. A piano stood in the rumpus room, to finish the impression of the Victorian era decor, though neither the husband nor the wife could play the grand old instrument.

The couple could never spare time to learn music, but they never forgot to use cutlery and napkins on the dining table. They remembered at all times not to speak in Hindi amongst themselves. They derived their sense of worth from making the acquaintance of people of English descent and the browns were strategically eliminated from their social contacts. Hence Yashoda grew up in a cauldron of cultures, religions, and values. Influenced by multiple worlds, she grew up to be a wonderfully mystical girl.

In her new life Yashoda was bestowed with rare beauty. She was given all that a girl may desire: a delicate figure and pleasant looks, peaches-and-cream complexion and a supple body, and all the assets that make one girl more desirable than the other. Her eyes were a misty brown and raven hair complemented her pink skin. Her parents marvelled at her extraordinary beauty. Ordinarily plain-looking that they were, this beautiful creation seemed to them a handiwork of Gods.

The year before Yashoda's birth, rumours of all sorts had been rife in their Indian neighbourhood. The neighbours claimed that they had seen an English man sneak into the house when Maya's husband was away at work. There were stories about how Maya's wardrobe had changed overnight after the arrival of a lover. Though her mother vehemently rubbished all talk of adultery as malicious gossip, her father either ignored or condoned it. Maya could never be sure how much her husband had known of her affair and if at all he suspected infidelity. All through her life she maintained that the set of Indian neighbours were jealous of her lifestyle and English connections.

"They are just a vituperative lot of Indians who want to be included in my circle! But you can't make friends out of neighbours, can you?"

Maya's lover died soon after his love child was born, happy in the knowledge that he had passed his love for poetry to a new soul. He had had little success as a poet and a lover. He lamented, in his last days, that he had not been given his due.

'I deserved a better life! I have given my art everything that a man can and I have loved, whenever I did, every one of the women, with all my heart.' He died at a young age of 33 with as many loves behind him and a tome of 3,000 poems.

'The pain of failure is sometimes too much to bear,' he wrote. When he sensed his end approaching, he walked in the freezing

London winter to Maya's flower shop. In her safe custody he left all his poetry, his life's pain and toil.

"Share it with my daughter when she grows up; tell her of my love for a child I couldn't call my own. Just this one thing, I ask of you Maya." He died that night from prolonged exposure to cold.

Maya had been unable to conceive a child with her husband. She had fallen in love, after being married for a good five years, with a poor English poet. Perhaps it was the love for all things 'white' or the shame of being a brown that she could not resist the amorous love of a white man. Or maybe it was Hollywood conditioning that trains human senses, worldwide, to desire certain physiological traits over the others, which had prompted her to stray out of a happy marriage. But she had loved, however briefly, in all honesty. However, Maya was too Indian to leave a husband for a lover, too smart to give up financial comfort for penury, and yet she had been passionate enough to follow her heart and love a man outside marriage.

Rose had seemed a perfect name for the rosy, bouncing baby born to Maya. Maya had wanted a Christian name for her child and when the baby arrived, everyone concurred on a name that best described her beauty. The baby 'Yashoda' weighed six pounds at birth. Her legs were so plump that she couldn't sway them for too long without tiring. Her fat cheeks came up to her chin and her chin rested on the folds of fat around her neck; in all she was a big, fat child bordering on obesity. Maya's husband imagined that his daughter resembled his own mother and he took pains to point out the lineage to all the visitors. In Edmonton, no one could have known what his mother had looked like, in India, some 40 years ago.

As is with pretty girls, Rose had many suitors when she came of age. However, unlike girls of her age, Rose had little interest in boys or sex. She had a calling that she failed to put her finger on; it was a calling of the soul. Her days were spent watching birds fly, walking by the brook, and pouring over books. The day Rose turned 16 her mother took out a hardbound book, covered in a silk cloth, from the drawer of her desk in the flower shop.

"These poems were given to me by a friend who was a poet. They were handwritten initially but I typed them out to preserve them for you. There's only one copy of his poems in the world, the one you hold in your hands. You see it is a precious book, not only because it was written by a talented man who died in obscurity, but also because he was extremely fond of you, my princess. He left his life's work in my custody so that I would pass it on to you. Now that you are old enough to look after things and are fond of writing too, so I thought that the time had come to hand it over to the rightful owner. You must think of that poet as your father because I think it was he that sowed the seed of poetry in your soul. It is his spirit that lives on through you."

From then onwards, Rose lived a life of mystical existence, a life devoted to poetry and connecting with a dead poet. She often walked to the cemetery, where he lay, with fresh flowers from her mother's shop. She read aloud his poetry to the birds in her backyard and shared his works on social media sites and with friends at school. She wondered what he had looked like and why he had written what he had. Why had he suffered, why had he been rejected in love? She wept as she read his words.

'Upon posterity a poet gets his due,' read an article carrying a brief note about the anonymous poet and his works. He soon came to be referred to as Rose's mentor. And with Rose, as his self-appointed literary agent, the poet came to life posthumously.

One day, not too long after her 16th birthday, Rose met a young English lad at the cemetery where her biological father was buried. She took it upon herself to look after this young orphan who had come with his uncle to lay a wreath upon his parents' graves. Rose lived in a state of mystical connection with the Universe and to her their meeting was not a chance event, it was a cosmic design, she insisted.

As for the lad, he had never seen a lass so beautiful and tender. He was moved by her beauty and kindness. And in the year 2036, when the world had moved away from real to virtual love, two lovers recreated the love of Victorian times. They were often sighted walking arm in arm in the lawns, or sitting on a bench reading poetry. They would spend hours talking on the church steps, or simply gazing at the sky and whistling to the birds. Their world was charming and mystical, cut off from the rest.

On one such day when the lovers were walking up the steps, their arms linked and eyes never betraying each other's gaze (they forgot to blink at times, such was their longing for each other), Rose sighted an old man. He was descending the church steps feebly and with trepidation. Without a thought to her lover, Rose darted to help the man who seemed almost blind. She offered her arm and helped him to the gate.

"Can I drop you somewhere?" she asked the old man.

"You have done your bit, Rose, the beautiful flower. Now go, run to your beau, he's waiting for you."

"How do you know my name? How do you know what I look like? You can't even see the next step! Do you know me from somewhere?"

"From many lives, Rose. I had promised to visit you in this life and I am here to keep my promise. This is your life of abundance, my dear. Touch as many lives as you can with your kindness. You have been given all, but do not turn selfish and arrogant. Share your bread, shower your love, and be the virtuous woman that you have always been. And remember, I am always by your side, even when you don't see me."

The old man faded into nothingness.

"Don't know what happened, ma'am. She was walking up the steps of the church with me as I narrated William Blake. We were engrossed in the moment when all of a sudden she dropped my hand and ran to something or someone. Though I could see nothing, she behaved as if someone was there. She disregarded me completely. It seemed to me that she was helping someone down the stairs. I called out to her but she took no notice. She slighted me, or so I thought then. On reaching the gate of the church she stopped and stood all by herself, talking excitedly, and then just as suddenly she fainted." The young boy, who was as shocked as Rose after the incident, narrated the episode in poetic detail to her parents.

Thereafter Rose and her boyfriend were forbidden by the elders from going to the cemetery or even the church. For a few years Rose lived in the belief that she had met a spirit on the steps of the church. But with time and on others' persuasion, she expunged the experience from her memory.

Krishna met Rose several times during her lifetime but she failed to see him for what he was, just as we all fail to see the mystical presence in our lives.

Life went on, as it does.

Life also continued for Sunderaman.

He had taken the advice that had been given and decided to take a long look at himself. At least he was not a dog now although he did appear to be big and fat and in a way, greasy.

Sunderaman decided that it was time for a change and at the centre of it would be he himself. He had already started a sort of fitness regime as he walked his puppies daily. He had other plans too. He had decided to make his wife happy and off he went to the Hanuman Temple at Connaught Place where he pledged his life to her.

So it was on a fine Monday morning, that Sunderaman began his new life. He tethered all his pups and the mother dog to their leads and then started to run through the streets. People cheered as they saw him pass. Some would say, "Good old Sunderaman, he has changed now and often leaves a few coins as he passes."

Others would say, "Look at that fat rolling ball of a man with his pack of dogs, he is mad, do you see that as he runs sometimes his coins fall from his pockets."

Most were pleased to see him, though. As he ran, children especially would cheer and smile. Some kids used to pelt him with stones in the early days of his experiment that came to be called 'Finding Sunderaman of Old'. Sunderaman ignored those angry urchins who called him names, jeered at his paunch, and made humiliating remarks about his age and size. He ignored their stones, as did his dogs, and after a couple of weeks the angry children of the streets gave up on him. Some even joined him in his run.

Sunderaman loved to watch the children play with the pups. Sunderaman stopped to take rest and feed the dogs in the middle of his long run. He watched children play with his dogs while he sat and relaxed. A few coins fell from his pockets at the place where he sat and the children were always grateful for these. One small child felt guilty at retrieving a coin though and had kept it to give it back to Sunderaman the next time he passed.

"You dropped this coin," said the boy to Sunderaman, "I have kept it so that I can return it to you."

Sunderaman smiled as he took the coin, he then handed over a bigger, brighter coin and said, "I always drop a few my boy but it is deliberate. I have more than enough wealth and it is just my way of giving. As long as you appreciate the coins and as long as you help anyone that needs helping in this life, then I am happy." He then ran off again with his dogs at his heels.

Back home, his wife was sometimes hard pressed not to berate him and ask where all his pocket money had gone but she knew that he had a few more coins salted away. She could not but help smile as she saw him returning home these days. He had been running daily now for many months, his temper had cooled and he appeared to be dedicated to her. The running had brought about a change in him, he had lost weight and even looked younger. She smiled at the thought of how his prowess in the bedroom had also returned. 'Enough of those thoughts,' she said to herself.

"Do you hear me, Laxmi's father; dinner is almost ready," she would call to him without uttering his name. It was customary in their village to not call the husband directly by his name or even utter his name without a suffix of respect.

"And have you laid out the bowls for the dogs, my better half?" asked her husband.

"Of course, what choice do I have?" came the angry reply.

Sunderaman smiled at her, "You don't have to do it my beautiful wife, if you don't want to. They are my headache!"

His wife smiled and replied, "And you are mine!"

Sunderaman had found his place in life. He realized that he was older now and it was not worth his while to be either chasing young women or chasing wealth. He gave up working at the hospital long ago and now did some voluntary work at the very hospital where he had been a corrupt employee for years. He had kept the bag that Old Nick had left him and every so often he would open it to take out a few coins (this bag seemed to be a never-ending pool of coins), and scatter them where needed. Even Old Nick was now helping out the poor although he did not know it. He was now very happy in his life.

Gods were watching though. Buddy Roy would often use his third eye, as he continued his search for the perfect floatation, to gaze down on Sunderaman.

'That is one human who is coming along nicely,' he would tell himself.

He also sometimes looked at the computer program that he had made for Old Nick, although he was very quiet and careful when he did this. As he gazed down he saw the madness and the turmoil that occurred, he also saw that Old Nick was quite happy and was smiling to himself. Even in this virtual world, everything seemed to be perfect.

He would sometimes gaze upon Krishna and Chris, just to ensure that they were going about their Godly duties in the correct fashion but what he liked most of all was to join them on the Facebook page and enjoy the conversation in their chat room.

Life, well eternity, was indeed good.

OHH! GODS ARE ONLINE..

୫୦

It is a strange world indeed. At one time or another, many thousands will be sitting alone as they gaze at the computer screen before them. Alone, but not alone, as they are all now connected with one another by the Internet. Is this an invention by man or is it something that was ordained by the Gods? After all, all Gods really want is for us all to be joined in harmony together. One people, one great big puzzle that is joined together with no pieces missing, for if just one piece is missing then the whole picture cannot be seen.

The Internet is just the start of this one big puzzle and one day everyone will be a part of it and on that one momentous day, everyone will be online together, including Gods.

Facebook, Twitter, Linkedin, Railchat, NetOrbis and scores of other social media sites to make it possible.

But on this one little occasion Chris looked at his computer screen as he logged in and seeing his old friend Krishna online, he started to type a message.

"Hello."

Krishna saw the message and replied.

"Hello, my brother, how are you?"

Buddy Roy watched from the sidelines ready to join in, as and when he thought he was required.

"Buddy is waiting to chat with you, Chris. Ohh! Gods are online, today. I can see Vishnu, Kamdev, and Aphrodite, on chat. I suppose they are helping people fall in love online," Krishna teased his friends.

"Not me, I am happy to watch you two. And what are we arguing about tonight?"

"I think we ought to promote ourselves on Facebook, mates, what do you say? Everyone has a page or a group of followers, even the non-believers have a group!"

"Not so soon Krishna, don't jump onto the wagon so soon. Wait for a year and you will see another social media fad, wait for a year to go by."

"I wish to reward all those who keep off social media," re-joined Buddy Roy.

"I bet all the monks in your monastery will qualify for the reward."

Weren't the Gods in a mood to jest that day?

"But really, I am tired of all this social networking business. Why can't human beings connect with their relatives, neighbours, friends, and all the real people in their lives and yes, even with their Gods? Why can't they smile at their fellow passengers? Why don't they ever notice the guy sitting on the seat next to them on the local train? And this, even though, they have been travelling together for years on the same train, day after day? Really, human beings surprise me no end!"

Krishna expressed his disappointment as other Gods heard him out, not interjecting, not even trying to gainsay his line of argument. They nodded in assent and typed 'I know' in the chat box.

"But we are all slaves to our creations, aren't we, brother?" Chris typed a succinct reply.

Buddy Roy chuckled at his screen and Krishna felt he had been stumped.

"Are we?"Sarcasm had always been Krishna's style, and he would not allow Chris to win an argument easily.

"Look at us, Krishna, all of us, the so-called Gods. We could finish this Universe, with all its magnificence, in a split second; but we guard it. You, my brother, you live the life of a man; subject yourself to the vagaries of life like any ordinary human being, why do you think you do that? Because you love mankind, your creation, however flawed they may be, you own them. You want to save him even though you lament he is corrupt in his soul. In a way we are slaves to our own creation."

Buddy Roy intervened: "How about another party, guys? The Gods didn't have their fill last time!"

"Virtual or Real?" typed Chris and Krishna together.

The End

GLOSSARY OF HINDI, SANSKRIT, MALYALAM, MARATHI WORDS

ॐ

Chawl	A large building divided into many separate tenements, offering cheap, basic accommodation
Ayurveda	An ancient intricate medical system
Kalyuga	The age of vices
Sakhas	A friend, A beloved
Halwai	Sweet-maker
Burfi	An Indian sweet made from milk
Dharma	Ancient Hindu idea of propriety and duty
Parantha	A thick piece of unleavened bread fried on a griddle
Indralok	Heaven
Avatar	Incarnation
Karambhoomi	The land where one works
Chechi	Address for an elder sister in Malayalam
Lalaji	Address for a rich businessman
Kali	A Hindu Goddess assosciated with empowerment
Yugas	Time Division, An epoch or era within a cycle of 4 ages
Bhakti	Faith
Saheb	An address placed before a man's name as a mark of respect
Jawan	Soldier in the Indian Army
Karma	Universal principle of cause and effect
Kurukshetra	A city in Northern India famous for the battle fought between Pandavas and Kauravas.

Jehadi　　　An Arabic term meaning a man in the service of God

Duryodhana, Draupadi, Dushasana, and *Karna* are characters from the Mahabharata

Carnatic　　Music A system of music assosciated with Southern India

Abhigyana Shaakuntalam A great ancient Sanskrit play by Kalidasa

Samosas　　A deep fried pastry filled with potatoes etc.

Tandav　　　Shiva's vigorous dance that is the source of creation, preservation, and dissolution

Sewak　　　Volunteer

Baba ki jai!　Hail Baba!

Satyagraha　A form of non-violence resistance initiated by Mahatma Gandhi

Pranayam　　A Sanskrit word meaning extension of breath

Bhajans　　A type of Indian devotional song

Brahmachari Celibate

Hawaldar　　A non-commissioned officer in Indian army or police

Anulom-Vilom A type of breath exercise

Dharnas　　Public demonstration against establishment

Kurta-Pyjama A long-sleeved hip length shirt worn with a loose trouser

Ma　　　　　Address for mother

Pooris　　　A light unleavened Indian wheat bread, usually deep fried

Nirvana　　Personal liberation in Hindu religion

Janmashthmi Hindu festival to celebrate Krishna's birth

Parikarma　Circumambulation of sacred places in Hindu context

Kurus　　　Name of Indo-Aryan clan

Prasad　　An edible food first offered to deity and then distributed in his/her name to followers

Vasnas　　　Desires, Inclinations

Baba	An address for father in Urdu
Ammi	An address for mother in Urdu
Aarti	Hindu religious ritual of worship
Ghat	Steps leading to a water body
Ganga Aarti	Worship of river Ganges
Diyas	Earthen lamps
Gau Ghat	A religious place in Haridwar
Har Ki Pauri	A famous ghat on the banks of river Ganges
Dhaba	Small eating joint by roadside
Kachodis	A fried flaky Indian snack stuffed with lentils

Srishti's all time bestsellers ₹ 100 each

- A Dilli-Mumbai Love Story
- A Feeling Beyond Words
- A half baked love story
- A Little Bit of Love...
- A Little Love Incident
- And then it rained....
- A Roller Coaster Ride!
- As Long as I Love you...
- A thing beyond forever
- Because you Loved me..
- Beep you! you BeepHole
- Boundless Saga of Love
- Can't Cook a Love Story
- Corporate Atyaachaar
- Crazy Bloody Thing LOV
- Everything you Desire
- Few things left unsaid
- Heartbreaks & Dreams!
- I am Broke....! Love me
- I am Still Committed..
- If God went to B-School
- If I Pretend I am Sorry!
- It Happened that Night
- In Course of True Love
- It's all About Love...
- It Should Be u!! My Love

- It wasn't Love at First
- Jab se you have loved me
- Journey of two Hearts
- Life is What you Make it
- Love Happens Like that
- Love, Life & A Beer Can!
- Love, me and Bullshit!
- Love Power Politics!!
- Love a Rather Bad Idea
- LUV is a Dirty Business
- Nothing Lasts Forever
- Of Tattoos and Taboos!
- Oops! 'I' fell in Love!
- Ouch! that 'Hearts'..
- Patyala Down De Throat
- Plz.. Kiss me or Kill me
- She is Single I'm Taken
- 34 Bubblegums and Candies
- That Kiss in the Rain..
- The Idiot-Dudes.....
- The India I Dream of
- The Lost Scraps of Love
- The Off-Site Tamasha
- The Quest for Nothing!
- The Thing Between U & Me
- Those Small Lil Things

- Brain Building for achievement
- Cheiro's : Language of the Hand

- Winning Personality: